Brindaria

Copyright © 2013 by Chris Wall

All rights reserved.

Cover design by Chris Wall
Book design by Chris Wall

No part of this book may be reproduced in any form or by any electronic or mechanical means including information storage and retrieval systems, without permission in writing from the author. The only exception is by a reviewer, who may quote short excerpts in a review.

This book is a work of fiction. Names, characters, places, and incidents either are products of the author's imagination or are used fictitiously. Any resemblance to actual persons, living or dead, events, or locales is entirely coincidental.

ISBN-978-1-304-62082-8

"Magic is believing in yourself, if you can do that, you can make anything happen."

— Johann Wolfgang von Goethe

Prologue:

As a kid, I had always heard stories about magic and wizards. I remember there being days where I wished someone would come and take me away like Hagrid did for Harry Potter.

Well, what if I told you that such a thing could exist? What if I said that there was a world where that sort of stuff was real? Wizards, magic, damsels in distress; all real.

I was never a believer. I had always hoped, but never believed. Well I was made a believer.

It all started when I went to the mall with a few of my friends; that was when everything went to hell…

Chapter 1

I had been sitting on the living room couch, refreshing Facebook every five minutes out of sheer boredom. The room was small with one window that lit the trash covered floor. The grungy bit of carpet you *could* see was well accented by the worn out furniture; two sofas, a coffee stained coffee table, and a flat screen TV that didn't match its surroundings at all. I'd never complain about my living arrangements, my parents did what they could to keep a roof over our heads, but the mess only got worse the more they were at work.

Knocking echoed off the door. The door swung open to reveal my friends Kate, Kristen, and Colin. Kate and Kristen stifled small giggles as Colin shook his head.

"What?" I asked, looking from one face to the next.

"I didn't expect you to have any hair on your chest," Colin remarked. Kate and Kristen, who couldn't control themselves for another moment, burst into a fit of laughter.

I looked down to see that I wasn't wearing a shirt. I grabbed a blanket that had been draped over the couch and smiled. I felt my face reddening as I jogged down the hall into my bedroom to grab a shirt.

"Come on in, guys," I said sarcastically as I walked out into the living room. The trio had been making themselves at home; feet up on the table, shoes strewn about, and Colin had already raided the snack cabinet.

"What's up?" I asked, closing the door that they had left open.

"We wanted to see if you like to go to the mall with us?" Kristen asked.

I hesitated, on one hand I would have loved to go and hang out, but on the other hand there was something stopping me. See, Kate and Kristen were my two best friends, but they were also dating, so whenever we hung out I always felt like a third wheel. Sure, I loved the idea of them being happy but it got to be a little too much sometimes. Kate, always knowing what was bothering me, stepped up.

"Joe, come on," she said.

Kristen smiled and, in a cheery tone, said, "If you come we can go to Harrison's."

I sighed, knowing I'd regret going, but instead of refusing I said, "Alright, I'll go. Let me just go grab a sweatshirt or something."

Chapter 2

We got to the mall about half an hour later and we wandered around. We browsed a couple of different stores for at least an hour when we reached a middle kiosk between RadioShack and Build-a-Bear. I kind of walked off on my own, starting to get a little sick of the whole Kristen and Kate thing. I walked a full circle around the kiosk, and I realized that I couldn't find my friends.

I sighed and started walking, and as always my feet carried me to Harrison's Comics.

I sighed and thought, *This is why you don't have a girl, Joe.*

"Cool sweatshirt," a girl said as she walked out of the comic store, smiling as she went.

"Thanks," I said, looking down at my sweatshirt, the white star gleaming against the blue backdrop. It was designed to look like the Captain America costume; with the red and white stripes around the torso. When I pulled the hood on, the girl almost lost it, because it doubled as the Captain America mask; two eyeholes, a big white "A" on the forehead and a white wing on either side of my head.

"That is *so* cool!" She said, and then she looked over my shoulder. Her expression shifted. "I should go," she said, sounding disappointed. "Again, nice sweatshirt." She walked off and I turned to watch her go, and then I saw Kate standing almost directly behind me.

"No," I said, grief ridden. "No, she's just a friend! She doesn't even *like* men; she has a girlfriend!" It was too late, though, the girl was gone. "Cockblocked by a lesbian, oh the irony," I groaned.

"Sorry," Kate said, looking both embarrassed and amused.

"Don't be! She wasn't that pretty anyway," I lied, smiling a little.

"I lost Kristen and Colin, so I came looking for you. Why am I not surprised to find you here?" Kate asked. She looked around, making sure no one was listening, and then leaned in close and whispered, "Can we find a bathroom?"

"Yeah," I said, checking my phone for any new texts. "We can just tell them we're at a bathroom and hopefully we can meet up."

There was still no sign of Colin and Kristen anywhere by the time we got to the bathroom. The Mall of New Hampshire wasn't that big, but trying to find two people there was like trying to find a needle in a hay stack.

We got to the bathroom near Hot Topic, and Kate walked down the hall to the restroom. I went and sat down at the benches to wait for her. I checked my phone again; I had gotten a text message from Kristen. It was a picture of a stuffed bear dressed as Batman.

"Build-a-Bear," I muttered, rolling my eyes. I backed out of the message and pocketed the phone, when suddenly a loud boom echoed from the other side of the mall. I thought it was just thunder, Hurricane Sandy making her way above us, and then I saw the explosion. I got up, raced down the hall and banged on the ladies room door.

"Kate," I called. "You might wanna speed it up in there!" I raced back down hall in time to see that the renaissance faire was in town, a knight in full steel armor was coming around the corner. He brought his sword down on me but I dodged right, grabbed his arm and twisted the sword out of his hands. I stood with the heavy steel sword pointed at the man's jugular. "This is a *real* sword," I noted, eyes narrowing. "You were trying to *kill* me!"

"We were promised there would be no resistance," the man, or beast rather, growled as confusion crept into his voice.

"You were trying to *kill* me," I repeated, readying the sword.

"Yes," the man-beast said, standing tall.

"Then I'll have no remorse doing *this*," I pulled the sword back and shoved it into the chink of the man's armor and he howled in pain. Instead of bleeding, however, he crumpled to dust. I noticed the odor of rotting flesh shortly after. "Zombie knights… of course."

Kate ran down the hall in time to see me pulling the sword from the armor. "What's happening?" She asked, a twinkle of fear dancing in her eyes, like the bulb of a flashlight.

"Something is happening and it's not good," I said, poking my head around the corner to see the damage. "We need to find Colin and Kristen and get the hell out of here!" We charged across the hall to Hot Topic and I saw two knights, one was about to strike a woman, the other was watching. I looked in Hot Topic and found, ironically enough, a Captain America shield. I grabbed it and threw it at the man about to strike; it hit him in the head, denting the helmet.

The other knight, looking up to see me and Kate, drew his sword and charged. I grabbed another shield and blocked the slash – though the shield crumpled – and thrust my sword into the man's belly. He, too, crumpled to dust.

We ran along the hall until we reached the center of the mall where they had a whole Christmas display set up. I remembered wondering why they were rushing Christmas, it was only November. Now I counted it as a blessing because it meant that the knights couldn't see us from the other side. We ran down the hall and I slid to a stop in the doorway of RadioShack, which was right across the hall from Build-a-Bear.

"This is insane," I said more to myself than Kate. "What the hell is going on?" I looked across to see the red hair of my friend, and Kate's girlfriend, Kristen. When I pointed her out to Kate I could see some stress leaving her face.

"Come on," I said, checking to be sure the coast was clear. "Let's hop over there before we're seen." I sprinted across the hall with Kate on my heels. When we were safely across, I grabbed the gate that blocked the doors at closing time and yanked them closed with a *clang!* I locked the gate and closed the doors.

"There," I said turning, "that should…" I didn't get a chance to finish, because just as I turned my head I was able to raise my sword just as another came down. I kicked the knight in the chest, sending him tumbling back. As his sword clattered to the floor, mine was already piercing his heart. "*Son* of a bitch! I really wish they would stop *doing* that!"

"Joe!" Kristen exclaimed, apparently just realizing that he was the hero before her. "What's going on?!"

"Oh you know," I said with an air of sarcasm. "Zombie knights attacking and I'm knocking some heads in. Same old, same old! How are you?"

There was a bang from behind; I turned to see knights trying to get through the gate. I turned to one of the workers and asked, "Is there a back door to this place?"

The worker, clearly flustered, said, "Y-yeah, there's a door to a maintenance hall right this way." He gestured toward a door with a sign that said "Employees only."

"Fantastic," I said, picking up the sword of the fallen knight. I held it up and said to the group before me, "Someone take this and cover the rear of the group, that door won't hold them off forever."

After an athletic looking young man took the sword from me I led everyone into the maintenance hall. Obviously the zombies had no idea about this place, because it was completely deserted. I led the group along the hall slowly, there was an intersection ahead. Just because I didn't see any knights didn't mean there were none. When we got to the intersection I held my hand up, signaling that everyone should come to a halt. I poked my head around the corner to see a knight holding a girl in a dress by the arm.

"You're coming with me," the knight growled menacingly.

"Release me," the girl shouted. She tried to get away, but the knight must have had one strong grip, because his arm hardly moved.

I had seen enough, I told the group to stay where they were and walked around the corner.

"Oi, ugly!" I shouted. The knight turned to see who had spoken, and to my horror his visor was up. He really was a zombie; his skin was a sickly green, half decomposed and full of holes. His eyes had been glowing red like some old cheesy horror flick monster.

The zombie snarled and said, "What's this? We were told there would to be no interference! Surely the warlock could not be wrong!"

"That's what the last guy said," I told him. I held up my sword and said, "And I got his sword."

"You'll pay dearly for that," the knight said. He released the girl, who fell against the wall, and charged at me. I parried his attack and slammed my shoulder against his chest. He staggered back and recovered fast, but not fast enough, because I knocked the sword from his hand and bashed the hilt of my sword into his face. He fell back, probably regretting keeping his visor up, and I stabbed him in the gut. His face seemed to decompose instantly, and only a skull remained until finally it crumpled to dust.

I crouched down next to the girl and said, "Hey, are you alright?" But before she could answer I heard a whistling sound. I turned and smacked an arrow away with my sword and without even blinking I charged the knight who had fired the arrow. He was on the other side of the intersection, any closer and he would have seen the group I was with. The knight seemed to be trying to decide sword or arrow. By the time he had decided, I was already cutting off his head.

I waved to the group, telling them to follow. I returned to the girl, who was just starting to stand. I offered my hand and she took it, pulling herself up.

"Thank you," she said, her dazzling blue eyes meeting my hazel ones.

"No problem," I said, finding it hard not to notice how beautiful she was. Now that the threat level was back down to a minimum, I noticed that her dress wasn't your average fall dress. She was wearing a full-fledged *Cinderella* type dress. Her brown hair was pulled up in a bun, minus one strand that hung down over her eye as a result of her scuffle with the knight. "Who *are* you?"

"More importantly," the girl said, narrowing her eyes and taking a lap around me. "Who are *you*?"

"I'm Joe, Joe Christian."

"Well, Joe Christian, you certainly are remarkable," Cinderella said. "Obviously you're more than just the average man from this realm."

"And you're from?"

"Not around here, obviously," she said, indicating her wardrobe. "I am from another land, one ruled by a horrible, unruly man."

"I see, and I guess the Corpse Knights are after you?"

"Indeed they are," she said grimly. She looked at the fallen knight that had her in his grasp just moments ago. "The Army of the Dead."

"I see," I said, my eyes widening. "What do they want you for?"

"My blood," the girl said, sighing. "For it is my blood that can raise their master."

"Well if the Master hasn't risen, then who raised them?" I asked, liking this situation less and less.

"A warlock," the girl said. "Morgar," she practically spat the name. "He's the foulest, cruelest man in my realm. He's also the ruler of my land. He murdered my father and butchered my mother; my whole family is dead."

"What's your name," I asked, hoping to lighten this dark mood, but to no avail.

"I am Princess Aela," the girl said proudly. "My family ruled the land I hail from before Morgar came and murdered my father, and took the throne."

"I'm speaking to royalty," I said. "Wonderful. Well your Highness, let's take this show on the road, shall we?" I started to walk, the group and Aela started to follow.

"Pretty boy back there said the wizard promised no interference," I said. "As did the first knight I killed, how come this Morgar guy didn't see me coming?"

"The only way Morgar couldn't have seen you in his vision was if you were a very powerful wizard yourself," Aela said.

"Oh yeah," I said, sarcastically, "I'm a real Harry Potter. I'm not a wizard, sweetheart; I'm just your average Joe. I have work, I have stress, and I have school. I don't do magic or spells, and I don't usually make it a point to carry around sword!"

"Then why, pray tell, are you so gifted?" Aela remarked.

"Adrenaline," I said with a shrug.

"I don't think so," Colin piped up; I had almost forgotten the group was behind me. "Sure, adrenaline would have helped a little, but there's no way you could have taken out all those well trained warriors solely on adrenaline."

Aela looked at me with the ever-so classic, "I told you so" look. We got to a set of double doors and I opened one of them just enough to stick my head out. When I did, I was met with the drizzle of rain. I looked up and saw archers perched all over the place; and I saw bodies littering the parking lot; people trying to escape, no doubt, only to be taken out by Morgar's men.

"They couldn't have picked a worse time to attack," I said, staring at the storm clouds just as a crack of lightning lit the sky. "Hurricane Sandy's going crazy out there."

"This storm is of my design," Aela said, almost as if conjuring a hurricane was as simple as making a box of Mac 'n Cheese.

"Your *design*?" someone from behind asked.

"Yes," the Princess said, nodding. "It was my transport into your realm from mine."

"And the portal to your realm is…?"

"You would know it as the Bermuda Triangle."

"Oh, of course," I said, rolling my eyes. "And I'm sure you learned of this realm when airplanes and ships appeared on your shores?"

"If planes are giant metal birds designed to carry people; then yes. It is rumored that my ancestors arrived through that portal."

"Wonderful," I said, turning my attention back to the archers. "You know, I could use some of that magic you were saying I should have right now." As if on cue, my blade burst into flames. I shouted and held it out, afraid of being burned and shouted, "Extinguish! Extinguish!" The fire disappeared, leaving no more heat on my blade as there was before. I looked at the group, and out of all of them, Aela was the only one who didn't look completely horrified.

"What is it they say in this realm?" She asked, thinking hard. "'I told you so'?"

"No one likes a show off," I said, smirking a bit. I looked back outside, an idea forming in my head. "Say, Princess, you can make it rain… would you be able to make it rain something… flammable?"

"Like torch fluid?" Aela asked, cocking her head like a dog.

"Yes! But only over the roof of this building, I wouldn't want to hurt anybody in the city."

"I can try," Aela said, closing her eyes and concentrating hard. The rain stopped everywhere but over the Mall. I lit my blade again and stepped outside; I aimed it at the rain and sent a fireball up to the roof. Aela must have done something right, because the rain caught on fire.

I grinned and muttered, "I set fire to the rain."

The guy who was covering the rear called ahead, "We should move! I hear someone coming!"

I nodded and said to the group, "Well folks, it's been fun! But you should all get to your cars and get home A.S.A.P!"

Everyone stormed past, each thanking me for saving their lives, and they all scattered. My friends and I ran toward the food court, which was where we had parked. We all hopped into Colin's car and when he started her up he put her in reverse and pulled out of the parking spot. He flipped over to drive and slammed the pedal down, throwing us all back into our seats as he raced toward the exit.

I looked up at the roof of the mall, where the rain had stopped, and saw a man standing at the edge. He raised his sword and, as if through a mega phone, he shouted, "*I claim this building for Morgar!*" He slammed the blade of his sword into the roof and a beam of light shot into the air, and a dark curtain started to drape itself over the Mall. We had just barely reached the exit when the curtain touched down, completely shrouding the mall in darkness. We jumped onto the highway and flew toward Raymond, New Hampshire.

Aela, still watching the Mall, said, "That is what he plans to do to my realm. He'll scorch all wildlife, enslave my people, and shroud the world into darkness. Now he'll do the same to this world! I am a fool for coming here! A fool!" She threw her face into her hands and started to sob.

"Hey now," Kate said. "It's not your fault. You couldn't have known he'd follow you here."

"Listen here," I said to the Princess, "this is in no way your fault. I will *not* let this guy get to you, you hear me? I'll kill him myself," I said, trying to sound heroic. "Chop off his head in the name of your father, alright?"

Aela shook her head and sniffled. "That will do no good," she said. "You would have to stab him in the heart."

"The heart?" I said, thinking about a book I had read, in which a wizard would summon a spirit that would then possess the body, and the only way to kill it is to pierce its heart. "That's oddly specific."

"Morgar is a spirit," Aela explained. "He possessed a man from my realm, and now uses his power to suppress my people."

"Well who did he…?" I stopped my sentence there. "Murdered your father… took the throne… Morgar possessed your father, didn't he?"

"Yes," Aela said grimly. "My father was in the family crypts, mourning my grandfather, for it had been exactly fifteen years since his passing. The spirit must have been lurking in the crypt for some time, awaiting a body pure enough to take. When my father returned from the crypt I knew there was something wrong, his eyes were as red as the blood moon. Then he took my mother… I could have stopped him; I had been trained with a sword and magic by the best masters in the kingdom…"

"No one could have expected you to kill your own father," Kate said reassuringly.

"No one should be asked to do that," I agreed, nodding.

"It matters not, now," Aela said. "Morgar will destroy my world and yours if he succeeds in raising his Master."

"Who is this Master of his, anyway?" Kristen asked.

"He has many names," Aela said. "Many in this world call him Hades, Pluto, Lucifer, or Satan. My people only have one name for him, though: Obcasus. Legend has it he was once the most powerful, horrible beings on the Earth and the ruler of mankind. Then one day, the great wizard Merlin created a world where Obcasus would never be able to escape. Your people call it Hell, we call it Morakâr."

"How can we stop Morgar from raising Obcasus?" I asked the Princess, but she only shook her head.

"There is no way," she said, tears coming to her eyes again. "The only one who can stop Morgar from raising Obcasus is Merlin, and he's been missing for centuries!"

"Missing," Colin said, "not dead?"

"Merlin is the equivalent to your God. He cannot be killed. He is immortal and has the ability to shape reality around him. He could be your teacher or even your father and you wouldn't know it."

"Alright," I said, "so how do we find him?"

"There's a map," Aela recalled, though she seemed uncertain, lightning flashed and lit up her blue eyes like a camera flash. "From what my father told me, the map was left by Merlin. Only 'He Who Is Worthy' can use it. I never knew what he meant until I saw the map myself. It is completely blank."

"What, you mean there's no map or…?"

"That's the thing," Aela said, sitting up straight again. "There *is* a map, but it will only show itself to the one person that Merlin would deem worthy."

"Where's this map now?" Kristen asked skeptically.

Aela's excitement died instantly, she slumped back down and sighed. "It's in my bedroom… back in my realm."

"Alright, then let's go get it," I said, and everyone looked at me.

"You can't be serious," Kristen said. "We can't just go traveling to another dimension!"

"Oh, of course not," I said. "I would never ask you guys to come along, but I can't let Aela travel alone!"

"Why are you being so kind to me," Aela asked, as if she was more used to people being cruel to her. "Why be so kind to someone who has brought death to so many people?"

"Because," I started, but I faltered… why *was* I helping this girl? This girl who brought with her a massive storm that's killed hundreds of people. This girl who brought with her an army of dead knights. This girl who so obviously would have been better off on her own, fighting to survive in some remote area where, even if Morgar's men found her, no one else would be in danger. I should have been baffled, I should have doubted my ability to help her, and I should have just said "Hit the road, Jack." I should have let that knight take her, but I didn't. "Because if you die, Obcasus rises. Besides, what kind of man would I be if I let a pretty girl – *royalty* nonetheless – wander into the unknown alone?"

"Perhaps Mother was wrong," Aela said dreamily, "perhaps chivalry in this realm *isn't* dead."

Chapter 3

Colin dropped me and Aela off at my house and I opened the door to find my mom and dad sitting in the living room. When they saw me they jumped up, the same expression of worry on either of their faces.

"Joe what happened?" my mom exclaimed, as over protective as ever.

I picked up the television remote and changed the channel to WMUR, the news channel for New Hampshire. On the screen was the Mall of New Hampshire, or rather, the curtain of darkness draped over it.

"And though authorities have tried everything in their power to get through this shroud of darkness," said an off screen voice, *"they have failed. It seems as though everyone who was in the Mall at the time are now trapped inside. With no way of communicating with anyone on the inside, we have no way of knowing what has happened."*

"Oh my god," mom said. "Were you..." She seemed to just notice Aela standing behind me. "Who's this?"

"This is Aela," I said. "Listen, I know what you're going to say, but I need to go with her. There's something important that we need to do where she's from."

"The hell you are," dad said, aghast. "If you think we're just going to let you go and do something stupid…"

"Stupid, like saving the world?" I snapped. "If I don't help her we could literally have Hell on Earth."

My father, a man of many words, was speechless. My mom was getting ready to cry and I knew what was going to happen.

"Go," she said, surprising everyone. "Sleep now and go in the morning."

I watched as my mother got up and walked into her bedroom. When the door closed, I heard a soft sob from the other side.

I was so exhausted from the day I had just had; and the thought of what was to come made me even more tired. I led Aela down the hall, showed her to my bed, and grabbed the extra blanket from the foot of the mattress and laid on the floor.

Just before drifting to sleep, I heard Aela whisper, "Good night, Joe Christian. May Merlin guide your dreams."

Unfortunately, Merlin wasn't with me in my dreams…

Chapter 4

I was in a dark chamber that was hotter than a volcano, so hot that I felt like I might have actually been melting. There was a slight growl from deeper in the chamber, and then I realized I was standing at the edge of a deep dark pit. The only thing that was in my head at that moment was one word: *Tartarus*.

It had occurred to me that a lot of mythology and stories in our world was based off of real things from Aela's world. I was just about to take a step back when there was a great puff of smoke, and before me floated the upper body of what seemed to be a man.

This was no ordinary man of course, he had massive horns that curled like a rams, along with the tusks of a boar. He had four eyes and the torso of a dragon, topped off with huge bat-like wings. I didn't need an introduction to know who this beast was.

"Obcasus," I said bravely.

"That is right," Obcasus said slowly, as if English were a second language. "And you are the one who killed my men and escaped with the Princess."

"Yeah, that'd be me," I said.

"You have interfered too many times, boy. Surrender the Princess to me and I shall spare you and the ones you love."

"And we'll be what exactly? Your slaves?"

"My rising is inevitable. No one can stop me but Merlin, and he is long since passed."

"That's what the people of Aela's kingdom must have thought about you too," I noted. "When you fear someone, it's best to assume their dead."

"I fear *NO* man!" Obcasus boomed, shaking the cavern.

"Oh, I don't doubt it," I said. "But from what I hear, Merlin is no mere man."

"Nay," Obcasus said, shaking his head. "Merlin was a God among men; it was what mother loved most about him."

"I'm sorry," I said, snorting. "'Mother'? You mean to tell me that you and Merlin are…"

"Brothers," Obcasus nodded. "Just as your St. Michael and Lucifer were brothers, Merlin and I share the same blood."

"Which is why he is the only one who can stop you," I said, putting two and two together.

"Yes," Obcasus said, suddenly he seemed to realize what was happening and he slammed his fist against the wall. "No more stalling, Joe Christian of New Hampshire. Will you turn over the Princess?"

"I'll turn her over," I agreed. "Right after Hell freezes over. Enjoy your stay in Cassa de Morakâr!"

Obcasus bellowed like a wildebeest, but it was too late, I was already waking up…

Chapter 5

The next morning Aela and I stepped outside onto the porch. She turned to me and said, "Are you sure you are up to this?"

I said, "Oh yeah, it'll be... fun."

She reached out her hand and said, "Fun indeed, I've never had a passenger before."

"Thanks," I said, my voice shaking slightly. "That's so reassuring."

"Hold on tight, sir knight," Aela said with what sounded like a flirtatious tone. Though, before I could inquire into it more we were whisked away in the wind.

It felt like just a few seconds before my feet touched solid ground. Solid being a loose term, because I was standing in sand. We had landed on a beach.

"Welcome, Joe Christian," Aela said, sweeping her hand across the landscape. "This is my home; this is Brindaria."

I looked in awe; this place was as beautiful as the Garden of Eden itself. The colors all meshed perfectly, while birds chirped in harmony. The only thing that didn't match this beautiful scenery was the rotund man standing about 10 feet from us.

"Master Arec!" Aela called, holding a hand up in greeting. She ran to the man and hugged him like he was an old relative… a very *short* old relative. "Joe, I would like to introduce to you the man who taught me everything I know, Arec."

"Nice to meet ya, lad," the dwarf man said.

"You're a… dwarf." I noted awkwardly.

"Aye," Arec said, narrowing his eyes. "Is that a problem?"

Noticing I had offended him I shook my head wildly and said, "No… God no! Sorry, where I'm from we don't have dwarves like you…"

"Ah," Arec said with a look of distaste on his face. "You're from *there*. You brought a human from the other side, eh?"

"If it weren't for this *human* I wouldn't have made it back here alive," Aela explained with more admiration than was necessary. "And I'm sure Obcasus would be wreaking havoc."

Arec grunted and nodded at my clothes. "What in the name of Merlin are you wearing, boy?"

I looked down at my tattered sweatshirt and jeans. I said, "They're the clothes of my people?"

"Those won't do you any good here," Arec said. "Come along, I'll get you some new armor." I followed the squat man to a hut that was reminiscent of the groundskeeper's hut from a childhood book.

Arec opened up a chest that was almost as tall as he was. He hopped up to dig inside. I was ready to grab his waistband in case he fell in, but he fell back onto his feet with some metal and leather. "Now," Arec said looking me up and down. "Are you going to want to keep the star and stripes?"

I thought about that for a moment, it would be cool to save the world as my favorite superhero. I nodded and said, "Yeah, that'd be great. Also," I revealed the shield I had grabbed from Hot Topic, which was in tatters, "I may need a new shield."

"Consider it done, lad," Arec said. "Any friend of the Princess is a friend o' mine. This will be ready for you in a few hours. You are free to relax until then."

"I was hoping to get started right away," Aela said as we walked back out to the beach. "But Arec is right; you won't get far dressed in your usual attire. I suppose waiting a little longer can't hurt."

"They won't get any farther in their plans, either," I pointed out. "They can't do much without you."

"This is true," Aela said, she laid out on the beach and stared up at the sky. It was a clear blue day, which was a nice change after dealing with Sandy. I stretched out next to her and couldn't help noticing how peaceful it was here; an environment untouched by the

Industrial Revolution. It was so peaceful in fact that it had felt like mere minutes had gone by when Arec hollered from his hut.

I looked over at Aela; she was sound asleep, not even fazed by Arec's call. I draped my almost ruined sweatshirt over her as a blanket and marched up to Arec's hut. When I got there he stood at the doorway with a quizzical look in Aela's direction.

"Sleeping," I said, following his gaze. "Is it done?"

"Sure is," Arec said. He puffed out his chest and said, "My best work if I do say so myself." He turned and walked into the hut and I followed. He stood aside, grabbed the tablecloth that had been draped over his project and pulled it off for the big reveal.

If it were possible for the human jaw to drop to the floor, mine sure would have. Before me was the armor that you would see in any artistic representation of a knight, the full steel torso with the steel legging, but it wasn't the armor that struck me, it was the color of the armor. Somehow Arec had been able to change the color of the metal accordingly to the color of my sweatshirt, though I saw no paint. The whole suit was blue, but on the chest was a large white star and below that were vertical red and white stripes that wrapped around the waistline of the armor. Beside it laid a helmet – not a full faced helmet, but it would give ample protection – with an "A" on the forehead, along with a white wing on either side of the head. And there, resting at the boots of the armor was the shield. The red and white rimmed around the blue circle with a white star in the middle. It shined like a freshly washed plate.

My look must have been quite amusing, because Arec chuckled and said, "You like it then, eh lad?"

"Like it?" I whispered. "It's amazing! How did you get the metal this color?"

"Old Dwarven secret," Arec said proudly. "You humans heat the metal and then cover your work in *paint*. Dwarves want people to see the detail in their work. Besides, paint wears off, but the colors will never run on this armor."

I was truly impressed, Arec gave me a minute to change; he walked out through the back door to water the garden he kept outside. I grabbed the suit and started putting on the gauntlets and I pulled on the chainmail. The breastplate was a little harder to do on my own, but finally I managed and when I finally got the steel on it felt lighter than air. At first, I thought Arec was pulling one over on me, giving me weak metal so I would die quick or something. But my suspicions were put on hold when I heard a scream from outside. I quickly put on my helmet, grabbed the shield and sword and rushed outside.

Aela was being dragged off by two knights, who marched toward a chariot pulled by a skeletal horse. I charged the knights, the light armor hardly making so much as a *tink* as I went so that, by the time the knights noticed I was there, I was already on top of them.

I slashed at one knight, who fell easily, while the other was trying to get at his sword. I didn't even let him pull it out; I slashed off his hand and kicked him in the chest. He fell backward onto the chariot; the rocking apparently made the skeletal horse think it was time to go, because it ran forward and took off with the one handed knight still in the chariot.

I helped Aela to her feet; her hair was a mess and she was covered in sand, though she still looked as beautiful as when I met her. I shook those thoughts out of my head; it was not the time to be thinking like that. I turned to see Arec hobbling over, wielding an axe in one hand and a watering can in the other. In place of his blacksmithing apron was a flowery pink apron that said, "Real men garden."

"I heard the scream," the dwarf panted. "What's happened?"

"Morgar's men," Aela said grimly, she noticed my armor and said, "We're ready to leave then, I presume?"

"Yeah," I said, nodding. "It's probably best that we get out of here before they return."

"Well if this is what you're adventure is going to be like, I want in!" Arec said, waving the watering can like a madman.

"We'd be honored to have you join us," Aela said, trying to suppress a smile at this truly terrifying sight.

"Good, I was going to come whether you liked it or not," Arec said, grinning behind his great beard.

"A kid, a Princess, and a dwarf," I said, lifting my sword up so that that the blade rested on my shoulder. "What could possibly go wrong?"

We all looked at each other and realized that there may be someone among us who won't make it back.

We started off toward the forest, which was dark and mysterious, probably filled with creatures able to tear each of us apart, limb from limb, at the same time.

I looked at the two people I was with and I thought, *We could do this*.

We walked into the woods – dwarf, Princess and knight – ready to take on one of the most evil men in this world. This time yesterday I was just an average Joe, and now? I'm on a quest to save the world with a beautiful girl and a crazy garden Dwarf. What more could a guy ask for?

Chapter 6

"Wow," I said, as we stepped into a clearing that had been at least a mile across, giving us a view of the castle, which was atop a hill.

"Yeah," Aela said, clearly holding back tears.

"So where's your room?" I asked, squinting to get a better look.

"The very top floor," Aela said.

"Oh, of course," I muttered. "Why is it always the top floor?"

"Father always was rather over protective," Aela said absently.

"That's an understatement," Arec grumbled, rolling his eyes.

"Why are there so many clearings in these woods?" I asked, since this was the second clearing we had entered.

"Many people lived in these woods," Aela explained. "When Morgar took over, all who didn't join him were banished from the world of the living. He erased all traces of life in this realm.

"Only reason I avoided such a fate was because my hut once belonged to a powerful wizard," Arec explained. "I don't think there's a man alive who could destroy my property."

We stood silent for a moment, giving our respects to those who had lived here.

"Come on," I said, breaking the silence. I started to walk toward the other side of the clearing. I got about halfway across when I got hit in the chest. I landed on my back but when I sat up I couldn't see anything, I stood up but was pushed back down again. "What the…?"

I heard the sound of a sword being drawn from its sheath and looked up to see Aela with her blade drawn. "Faeles," She said, going back to back with Arec.

"Faeles?" I asked, confused.

As if to answer my question, a group of wild looking cats appeared out of thin air.

"Faeles… cats," I muttered.

I surveyed the scene; these weren't the cats you'd see curled up on a couch. These cats were horrifying. Their eyes were glowing red, their fur was black with red streaks, and their teeth were ragged and broken. When they spoke their teeth wiggled in their gums. They smiled too, like that *loveable* character in the Disney film. There was something spine-chilling about a smiling cat. Even worse, when they smiled there was no humor in their eyes, only bloodlust.

I hopped up and ran to the other two, the cats started to move in a little bit. "Ooh, the Princess returns with a human. Lord Morgar will be more than happy to see you."

"Away with you, cat," Arec yelled. "Don't make me angry!"

"Quiet, dwarf, your kind hasn't had any significance in this realm since the death of the King."

"Why you little," Arec's face was growing even more red by the minute, soon his face was going to match the shade of his red beard.

"Arec please," Aela hissed. "Now is not the time." Arec grumbled something about how warm cat pelts were but said nothing after that. Aela stepped forward and said, "Faeles, our people have no quarrel. We have always been a peaceful pairing, why are you so adamant about turning us in?"

"Let's just say we were promised something in exchange for your life," the biggest of the Faeles said in a smooth, sly voice.

"And you trust Morgar?" I asked skeptically. "He's a snake, pussycat. He'll get what he wants and then when he no longer needs you he'll feed you to a hellhound or something."

"Do not speak on matters you know nothing about," the lead Faeles snapped. "He may seem untrustworthy, but we know he is telling us the truth."

"Really?" Aela asked. "Because he once told me something that I *thought* sounded like the truth. He told me that there would be peace and prosperity forever more under his reign; all I had to do was stand at his side. You know what happened after that? He tried to kill me."

"Not *kill*," the cat said, "*sacrifice!*"

"Same thing," Arec snapped. "The point is that the man was about to kill another person. Murder is murder, whether it's a sacrifice or not."

"And what of you, dwarf?" a different Faeles purred. "How many people have you killed in your lifetime?"

"They threatened what was mine," Arec defended.

"*Murder is murder*," the cat mocked.

"I… you… but…" Arec was sputtering and couldn't seem to put a coherent sentence together.

"What should we do," I whispered to Aela.

"I have a plan," Aela whispered back, her voice shaking.

"What's that?"

"Improvise?"

"Joy," I said, my spirits sinking. Here we were surrounded by floating, smiling cats with a taste for blood with no plan. I thought our goose was cooked until there was a rustling in the bushes and an arrow shot out and pinned two Faeles against a tree by their tails. The other cats whipped around toward the bush where the arrow came from, but another shot from a different bush pinned three more to a tree.

"What is happening?" the leader shouted, no longer wearing that wide, creepy smile.

"This is happening," a voice shouted from above, and we all looked up to see a hooded figure swoop down and kick the leader of the Faeles in the head. The cat landed on its feet – of course it did – and gaped at the girl. "This is impossible, the curse…"

"The curse says I cannot kill," the girl said, smirking from underneath her hood. "But I can still maim."

"Retreat!" the leader shouted to his comrades, until he realized that he had no more remaining forces whose tails were free. The cat looked back at the hooded figure and grimaced. He hissed, "Until next time, girl." And the leader disappeared.

"Who is *that*," I asked, awestruck.

"There is only one person in all of Brindaria who could do such feats with a bow and arrow," Aela said, walking toward the hooded wonder. She pulled the hood down to reveal a girl with dark skin, her eyes were hazel and her hair was curly. She had a dazzling smile and slight dimples. "Aurora Hayfield."

"Hello Aela," Aurora said. She had an indifferent tone of voice, like everything was just a game and she knew how to play it.

"Who's this?" I whispered to Arec.

"Aurora Hayfield," Arec said, nodding his head. "She was a hired sword for many years, starting at the age of nine, poor girl."

"And what about this curse the cat mentioned?"

"Well according to legend," Arec said, as if he'd told the story a thousand times, "when she hit the age of seventeen she was given a target to kill. But when she approached the old hag it turned out she was a witch. She cursed Aurora so that she could never take the life of another living thing, for risk of killing herself."

"So if she were to kill someone she would die as well," I recapped. "An assassin who can't kill."

"And who is this?" Aurora asked, eyeing me like she was trying to decide whether or not I was worth the effort.

"This is Joe Christian," Aela said informally, as if she were talking to an old friend. "He saved my life when I escaped to the other realm."

"Oh," Aurora said, suddenly very fascinated. "The *other* realm. Very nice." She winked at me and I could feel my face growing hot.

"Yes," Aela said, her smile seemed to falter, as if she were a small child witnessing someone plotting to take her favorite toy.

"So where are you all off to?" Aurora asked, still not taking her eyes off me.

"The castle," Aela said ominously. "We're going to find Merlin."

"Merlin," Aurora laughed. "You still believe in fairy tales, do you?"

"I must admit, I did not until very recently. Now with Morgar's rise to power, and all these crazy things happening…"

"Yes, it *is* good to hope," Aurora said with a bored tone. "What do *you* think about all this, Joe?"

Everyone looked to me like I was the deciding vote on what's real and what's fake. I just shook my head, however, and said, "Well, I never once believed any of *this* could be real. Wizards, dwarves, floating, invisible cats… why not Merlin?"

Aela smiled; obviously glad to see that I didn't think she was an idiot. Aurora seemed to consider this until finally she just shrugged her shoulders and said, "Well, I could never believe any of this, but if you all think it could save the kingdom, therefore my own hide, I would love to join you."

"Well actually," Aela started, but Arec jumped in, saying, "Of course! It would be great having a trained killer on the team; an assassin is always helpful when trying to sneak into a castle."

"It's true," I said. "Besides, if worse comes to worst, her fighting skills may come in handy."

Aela looked rather disappointed, but when she caught me watching her reaction she put on a big smile and said, "Why, it would be an honor to have you with us Aurora!"

"Great," Aurora said, she marched forward and winked at me again as she walked by. She made a show of it as she went, too, swinging her hips from side to side seductively. "Let's get going!"

Arec and I stumbled forward, following her; Aela sighed and followed along, rolling her eyes.

Chapter 7

We had been walking through the dark woods for a while, Aurora had an arrow notched, Arec had his axe at the ready, and Aela and I both had our swords out. We were all expecting the worst, but what we *didn't* expect was what we saw in the next clearing.

We stepped out into the sun, expecting to see more woods ahead, but somehow we all must have lost track of time because the castle stood not a mile from our position. We all looked at each other, as if we were all thinking the same thing: "We can't be there already."

"Well," Arec said walking forward, "we aren't going to get there just by standing here."

Aurora put a hand out in front of him, stopping him in his tracks. She crouched down, picked up a rock, and threw it a few feet in front of our position. Instead of falling to the ground, though, it vanished. The image before us rippled like she had thrown the rock into water.

"An illusion of some sort," Aela said, sounding impressed.

"Aye," Aurora said, nodding. "I've seen this kind of magic before; lost a good friend to one of these once."

"What is it?" I asked as I picked up a stick about the length of my arm and poked the image; it rippled for a short time then became solid again.

"A mirage," Aurora said. She looked to me and saw my puzzled expression. "In your realm you have mirages in a desert, the heat playing tricks on your mind. Same basic concept, but this is much worse. The spell shows an image of where you want to be and when you run into it you get trapped in a world of pure darkness. Some say there are even small creatures in there, hungry little buggers who want one thing and one thing only… flesh."

"They also say that there's no way out," Arec noted. "You go in and you're stuck in there forever; magic is completely absolved from a man. No one, not even Merlin himself, could use magic in a mirage."

"So what do we do?" Aela asked.

"We need to get around it somehow," Aurora said.

"Well then let's go," I said, lifting the branch and walking along the image. I dragged the branch along so that the image rippled as I went.

"Clever," Aurora complimented.

"What," I said, "you thought Aela only brought me along for my good looks?"

"Well," Aurora said with a flirtatious smile, while Aela blushed.

"Come on," I said, still dragging the stick along. After a while I looked to Aurora and asked, "How do you know so much about my world?"

"My friend," Aurora said. "He was from your world as well. We shared quite an adventure."

"What was his name?" I asked.

She looked at me, as if she were trying to figure out some puzzle.

Suddenly the stick stopped dragging along the mirage. I stepped forward, no darkness, just more woods. I looked to my right, the mirage was literally a flat image as thin as paper.

"Good call, lad," Arec said, patting me on the elbow. I'm sure that, if he were taller, it would have been a pat on the shoulder.

"All in a day's work," I said, I took another step forward and almost fell through the ground, but I caught solid dirt and scrambled to pull myself up.

"Joe!" Aela shrieked, she grabbed my arm and pulled, but it felt as if something were grabbing at my legs and trying to pull me through to the other side.

"Another mirage," Aurora said, cursing her own stupidity. "We're dealing with a very clever warlock."

"Indeed you are, my dear," came a voice from behind me, and from the look on Aela's face it could only be one man.

"Morgar," she squeaked.

"Hello Aela," Morgar said, his voice was smoother than I expected. It was like that one teacher you have whose voice makes you want to sleep. "I see your friend here wasn't smart enough to consider the fact that there may be a mirage on the ground."

"Hey," I snapped. "I'm plenty smart, alright?"

"Oh, I don't doubt it," Morgar said, his voice made my neck hair stand up on end; so calm, so emotionless.

"Why don't you let me up and I'll show you how smart I am," I challenged him. I couldn't see his reactions, to turn would involve releasing Aela's hands and those were the only anchors I had at the moment.

I heard him chuckle and then he said, "And by that I'm sure you don't mean you'll beat me in a game of chess?"

"Let him up," Aela begged.

"I shall," Morgar said; I could sense the humorless smile spread across his face. "When you agree to come with me with no strings attached."

"Don't do it, Aela," I said. "My life isn't worth you losing yours."

"I can't just let you die," Aela said, aghast.

"Oh come on, Princess," I said, smiling at her. "You really didn't think we'd all get out of this alive, did you?"

Her silence was an answer in itself. I looked to Arec, who looked as if he'd forgotten to water his posies. I said to the dwarf, "Take care of her, Arec. Don't let him get her."

The dwarf seemed to compose himself. He stood up straight and said, "Wouldn't dream of it, lad."

I nodded to him and looked at Aurora; she had this knowing look in her eyes, as if she knew this wasn't good bye. She just winked at me in that flirtatious way again. I smiled weakly at her, and I looked back at Aela, her blue eyes always filled me with warmth, but this time it filled me with something else; courage.

"Let go," I said. She seemed to find this shocking, as if she thought that the chick flick moment was all an act. "Let me go, Aela, before we both get pulled in."

She hesitated, and then she pulled herself closer and kissed me. Kissed by a Princess, how many guys can say they did that? She pulled back, tears running down her face… and she released me. I was pulled back hard, and everything went dark…

Chapter 8

I was waiting for whatever pulled me in to attack me, fully prepared to be torn to pieces and eaten by tiny little creatures. But nothing came, which filled my heart with dread. This meant one thing and one thing only; this was going to be a slow death. I've been doomed to float around here for the rest of my life. I didn't bother looking for a way out; Arec had said there was no escape from a mirage.

Instead, I thought about Aela, and about that kiss. Some part of me knew that she had feelings for me, but my low self-esteem kept pushing those thoughts out of my head.

She's a Princess, you'd be classified as a troll in this world, an inner voice hissed constantly. I shook my head; my self-esteem was the least of my problems.

My mind wandered back to Aela, as sure as I am alive that she's going to be devastated. After that kiss, it's obvious to me that she saw me as more than just potential help.

I was floating there for a good minute before something happened; the darkness shimmered and rippled and suddenly a picture opened up before me. It was Aela, Aurora, and Arec in that clearing.

Aela, who was still kneeing by the mirage I had fallen into, sobbed quietly. At the angle I was at I still couldn't see Morgar, but all I could picture was a horrid and grotesque face, grinning an evil, yellow grin.

"Well now that *that* nasty business is completed," Morgar said in his eerily calm voice. "Why don't you come with me, Princess?"

"Not a chance, warlock," Arec said, holding his axe as if he were about to throw it.

"You'll have to get though us, big, tall, and evil," Aurora said, looking rather bored but still kind of frightening.

"Oh, I plan on it," Morgar said. The mirage I fell through started to ripple, and I saw, to my surprise, Morgar was walking across the mirage like Jesus across water. Now I could see him, and what I saw was very surprising. He could have been handsome for an older guy, like Robert Downey Jr. or George Clooney. He had his jet black hair combed back in a sort of 1920s style; he had a goatee that came to a point at the bottom. He wore robes, much like wizards in old stories except these robes were as black as the dimension I was in.

Arec jumped in front of Aela, as a means of protecting her, but with just a flick of his wrist Morgar sent the dwarf flying across the clearing, into another mirage. I watched in horror as he took a hold of Aurora's throat and lifted her into the air with one hand. The color draining from her face, Aurora lowered her arm and a small blade protruded from her sleeve. She took a stab at Morgar but her vision must have been blurring because she missed her target but caught his left ear.

Morgar's emotionless grin turned into a scowl as he threw the assassin to the ground; she was out cold. He brought his hand up to his ear, blood trickling from between his fingers. He lifted his arm and a sword appeared in his fist. This was no mere steel sword though, it was jet black like his robes and seemed to glow with an evil power. He stood above Aurora, sword poised over her head, ready to make the final blow. He had murder in his eyes and was just about to strike when he was tackled from behind.

Arec had managed to crawl out from the mirage; he probably had a better hold on the ground than I had. Arec's height would have given him an advantage if he hadn't been so round. As it were, Arec made to grab the wizard's sword, but Morgar was too quick. He took a blind slash, and to my horror he had gotten lucky.

Arec stumbled back a few steps, holding his middle. Blood trickled from between his fingers just as it had on Morgar's ear just moments before. Arec fell to one knee, holding himself up with one hand while suppressing the blood with the other.

"Foolish dwarf," Morgar said, his smooth voice came out as a growl. He stood and turned to Arec, towering over his shorter yet bulkier foe. "You fight for a lost cause; I will kill you and then the assassin. Then I will kill the Princess you were sworn to protect and my master will rise and kill everything else."

"No," Arec grunted. "I still have faith."

"Faith?" Morgar laughed, spreading his arms. "Your cowardice Merlin cannot save you, dwarf. You are going to die and there is nothing anybody can do about it." He brought the sword up and Aela jumped up and grabbed his arm. Being delayed longer seemed to anger Morgar even more. He shouted and shoved the princess backward, and she tripped and hit her head on a rock. I felt anger welling up inside me, but what could I do? I was trapped in a mirage, never to see the light of day except through this damn window; but first, I would watch my friends die.

My anger got the best of me and I took a swing at the image, which rippled. Morgar looked in my direction, as if he had seen something. He seemed convinced that there was nothing there, though, because he turned back to Arec. I realized what had happened; I had reached back *into* the other world! I drew my sword and stepped through the portal.

"Take on last look around, Arec," Morgar said, holding the sword to the dwarf's throat. "All that you know is coming to an end."

Arec opened his eyes and looked around, and then he saw me. His eyes must have given something away, because Morgar whipped around, but too late. I swung my blade and took off his hand, causing his sword to drop to the ground and vanish. The pain must have diminished some of his power, because all of the mirages vanished and Morgar dropped to the ground, holding his arm like I had chopped off his hand or something... oh wait, I kind of did, didn't I?

Morgar looked at me like he had seen a ghost, which I'm sure he had seen plenty of times in his lifetime. I mean, hey, *he* was a spirit possessing a man. "How," he asked, fear filling his eyes. The first hint of emotion other than anger I've seen on his face.

"I found a back door," I said, smiling down at him. "And now I think it's time we parted ways, Morgar. But first you have to part ways with that heart of yours."

I went to stab the wizard, but his power must have been great before because he was able to jump aside and disappear in a cloud of smoke before my sword could have reached his heart. I cursed, how can I kill someone who could function like that with the pain of a sliced ear and missing hand?

I leaned down next to Arec, who was still bleeding out. His face was deathly pale and he was shaking all over.

"Is there anything I can do to help?" I asked him, knowing there was no way I could actually save him.

"Yeah," Arec said, falling onto his rear end. "You can stop crowding me. I'll be fine." Judging by the way his voice broke slightly and from the look in his eyes, I could see he knew that wasn't true. I decided I would back off, though, for his sake.

I got up and walked over to Aurora. I checked her pulse like I had seen on all those movies back home, she was still alive, so there was that. I walked over to Aela, she was bleeding a little on her head, but she the cut didn't look too bad. She probably had a slight concussion, though I couldn't really be sure. She was still breathing and her pulse seemed normal, she was just taking a little nap was all.

I walked back to Arec, he was lying down, almost perfectly still but when I sat his eyes opened and he looked at me. "How are the girls?"

"Alive," I said, I cringed at my own words. *Stupid*, I thought to myself.

"Good," Arec said, paying no mind to the stupidity of what I had said. "Listen, lad, there's something I wanted to say."

"Arec," I said, sighing. "Can we not do this? I really don't think…"

"I am a dying dwarf, let me have my final words," Arec said. He didn't say it in a mean tone, more like an exhausted tone, as if he were tired of people interrupting him. Tired of the world that interrupted his time at peace. "If you want to kill Morgar, you're going to need to be a lot stronger and a *lot* faster."

"I saw that," I said, remembering the handless, one-eared wonder making his escape.

"You need to train," Arec said. "You have potential, but if you don't practice you'll never stop what's coming."

"I don't have to," I said. "I just have to find Merlin and let him take over."

"You have to be deemed worthy," Arec said reminded me. "You'll be tested physically, mentally, and psychologically."

I sat there for a good five minutes, and then everything got quiet, including the rapid breaths that had been coming from beside me. I looked over at the great dwarf who had made me my armor and my blade just the day before; it seemed like a lifetime ago. His eyes were staring up at the heavens; I closed them with the heel of my hand. I sighed and looked around, wishing I had a shovel. I remembered Arec had packed a bag, I went and grabbed it. Sure enough, there was a shovel.

"Smart Garden Gnome," I whispered.

I started to dig; the sun had reached the tree line by the time I had the hole dug up.

I lowered the dwarf's body into the grave and laid his axe on his chest and crossed his arms. I then started to put the dirt back on his body. By the time I was done it was dark, I grabbed some sticks and brush and some thick branches. I piled them all up and lit my sword like I'd done at the mall. It was the first time I used this power since then. I started a fire and I sat down next to a rock that was big enough for a headstone and with the blade that never dulls I etched: "R.I.P Arec the Dwarf." I dropped it at the head of the grave and plopped down to my backside.

I let out a loud sigh and rubbed my eyes with my hands. I hadn't slept in almost twenty four hours, and if this was how it was going to be I doubted I would. I heard a groan from behind me and turned to see Aurora sitting up. She looked up at me next to the fire and her eyes flashed.

"Welcome back," she said, like she knew I would return the whole time.

"Thanks," I said, turning back to the grave. "I didn't get back in time, though."

Aurora noticed the broken earth and the rock and she took on a more solemn tone.

"It was inevitable," she said. "If Morgar didn't kill one of us then he would have just kept going. He wouldn't have given up as easily as he did; he's picking us off one by one."

"Yeah," I said, I picked up the wizard's hand from the ground and held it up. "I got a souvenir, though." The hand twitched, then came to life and jumped onto my shoulder. I jumped back and scrambled away from the hand. It fell to the ground and sat up on the palm. "What in the world?" I whispered, moving toward it.

The hand jumped up so that it was standing on its index and middle fingers, like it was standing on legs. It walked over to a stick and picked it up and wrote in the dirt. I summoned a small ball of fire and held it close to the etches in the dirt.

"Friend" was what it said.

"Oh my God," I said, realizing what was happening in front of me. "You're *king's* hand?" The hand gave me a thumbs-up. "So, what? Cutting you off cut off the connection to Morgar, and now you're the last bit of the King left?" The hand did a movement, somewhere between a shrug and a nod... if a hand could do either. "What do I call you?"

"What about Fives," Aurora offered, wiggling her five fingers.

The hand did a little back flip, apparently thrilled with the name.

"Fives it is, then," I said with a small smile.

"Why don't you sleep, Joe," Aurora said, moving to the fire. "I've rested enough; you should get some rest while you still can. I imagine that we'll reach the castle by midday tomorrow."

"I won't argue," I said. "If any trouble comes up, though, wake me."

"Don't worry," Aurora said, giving me one of her flirtatious smiles. "I'm a big girl." She winked and turned toward the fire. I laid down close to Aela, Fives jumped onto my chest and rolled into a fist; apparently that's how a hand sleeps. I closed my eyes and let the day's exhaustion overwhelm me...

Chapter 9

I woke up just before dawn, the sky was a very deep blue as the sun started to rise. I looked over at Aela, she was still out, but she seemed to be breathing normally. I looked up and saw that Aurora had fallen asleep. I got up and almost forgot about Fives, who fell with a jolt, but I caught him.

"Sorry," I whispered as Fives shook his fist at me. I walked over to Aurora and shook her awake; she jumped up and brandished a dagger, still half asleep.

"Easy," I said, holding my hands up. Fives jumped up like he was holding himself up.

"Sorry," Aurora said. "I don't know what happened; I guess I was more tired than I thought."

"Yeah," I said, nodding. "Come on, we should wake up the Princess and head out."

I walked over to Aela, who was sleeping like a baby. The blood had dried on her head but she still looked beautiful. I shook her shoulder and whispered her name. She moaned and started to stir; she put her hand on her head and opened her eyes. It took a moment for her to focus but when she did she looked up at me and her eyes grew wider than quarters.

"Joe," she said, lifting her hand to touch my cheek but stopped herself. "I'm dreaming, aren't I?"

"No," I said with a soft smile. "I'm one hundred percent real, Princess."

"Really?" She said, her eyes filling with tears of joy.

I knew I couldn't stall forever, so I just came right out with it and I said, "Aela… it's Arec."

She looked behind me and saw the grave and her tears of joy shifted to tears of sorrow.

"No," she said, shaking her head. "No."

"I'm sorry; I wish I could have stopped it but…"

Aela dropped her head onto my shoulder and sobbed for a good half hour. Finally she pulled herself together and wiped the tears from her eyes.

"We can't waste any more time," She said, standing. "We need to get to the castle and find Merlin before that monster kills anyone else."

She started toward the woods. Aurora and I looked at one another and the assassin shrugged and followed. I took one last look back at Arec's grave; we're off on our own without the old dwarf for the first time. Aela's had the guy there for her all her life, and now he was gone. It was no wonder she didn't want to stay, this *was* where it happened after all. I started walking, Fives sitting on my shoulder like a parrot on a pirate.

We walked for a while until finally we reached the end of the forest, and that was where the girls stopped. And I saw why when I caught up to them. We had finally reached the castle, but across a small field was the Army of the Dead sharpening swords and firing arrows for target practice.

"Well this is new," Aela said quietly.

"Really?" Aurora said, sarcastically. "You didn't have an army training right outside before you fled?"

"This isn't helping," I said, stepping between the girls. "We need to find a way to get through to the castle. A way that doesn't get us all killed," I added for Aurora's sake.

Aela looked over at me and her eyes got wide and she asked, "Joe, why do you have a hand on your shoulder?"

I looked at Fives and shook my head, "Not now. I'll explain later. Come on, we need to figure this out."

I walked along the tree line, all the way around the castle, but I saw no way through. What I *did* see, though, were a lot of explosives.

"If someone were to *misplace* their torch," I said, mind racing. "And the torch had *somehow* wound up next to the explosives…"

"It could blow a hole in their defense," Aurora said with a devious smile.

"And we could slip right in without anyone noticing," Aela finished, nodding her head.

"But who, oh who, could *possibly* sneak past *all* those knights?" I asked, looking at Fives with a sly smile. Fives jumped up on his index and middle fingers like they were legs and flexed his thumb and ring finger as if to say, "Bring it on, Captain!"

The little hand leapt from my shoulder and scuttled his way through the grass, which was so long that it completely covered him. For a time I couldn't see the hand, then I saw a torch hop out of its holder on the castle wall and bob toward the stacks of explosives. It all happened so fast that I didn't think Fives got out in time, the boxes and barrels all blew apart, sending wooden shrapnel into several of the knights. The ground and trees shook from the explosion and the knights all fell to the ground.

Under the cover of dust and smoke, Aela, Aurora, and I charged forward. We managed to get through to the castle with little difficulties, and we saw that the door was already open; and who do we see sitting on the handle?

"You clever little wonder," I said, grabbing Fives as I ran through the doorway. I charged through the main chambers. Empty.

I ran to a door that led to a staircase a few feet from the left of the throne, which stood as empty as the chamber. I rushed up the steps, taking two at a time, and when I reached the top I heard doors opening from behind. I turned in time to see a small group of undead running into the main chamber.

"We need to get up to your room fast, Princess," I said, pushing her in front of me so that she could lead the way through the castle.

"I'll hold off the rotters," Aurora said, drawing a sword.

"How?" I asked incredulously. "You can't kill!"

Aurora either forgot about that or just didn't really care, she waved off my comment and said, "I'll think of something. Just get to the tower and get that map!"

I was about to object but Aela grabbed my arm and said, "Joe, we can't waste any time, we have to move *now!*" I let her drag me away, I turned away from the assassin who couldn't kill and followed the Princess as we ran up stairs, stairs, and even more stairs. We took corners so quickly that we came close to slamming into the walls or tripping over tables topped with flowers.

We finally reached the top of the tower and when we charged through the door we met a *very* unfriendly sight.

Morgar was standing next to her bed. The room was completely trashed with paper, clothes, and jewelry that were littered across the floor. The wizard had his stump wrapped up in gauze and he looked very calm for someone who had gotten his hand cut off.

"Ah," the wizard said, extending his arms, "how kind of you to join me."

"Morgar," I said with an equal amount of calm on my face, but on the inside I was boiling. "Want me to take your other hand?"

"You got lucky, Christian," Morgar said with a smile that couldn't be trusted. "I didn't expect you to come out of that mirage. I won't underestimate you again, I assure you."

"You knew we would come here," Aela said, looking around. "Looks like you've redecorated."

"Yes," Morgar said, still smiling sweetly at them. That smile reminded me of a salesman about to make a sale, smiling but not because he's happy. He's smiling because he knows he has us right where he wants us. "And for the life of me," he said, "I can't seem to find that map that is *so* precious to you, my dear."

"Maybe because you're looking in all the wrong places," Aela said, smiling that same fake smile… she had a plan.

"Oh?" Morgar said, intrigued. "You've managed to put it in a spot where my magic could not see?"

"No," Aela said. "I put it in a place where your magic *could* see it but you chose to ignore it."

"What?" Morgar asked, his smile faltering.

Aela's eye snapped to a framed portrait of her and her father on her wall, Morgar seemed to catch her tell because he looked over and smiled wide again. He turned to the portrait and tore it off the wall, and while his back was turned Aela reached for a *different* portrait that depicted her and a woman who could only be her mother. She took the parchment out and folded it up and stuck it in her pocket. Meanwhile, Morgar was tearing through the picture, his smile now an ugly scowl, and his eyes glowed red with anger.

The wizard turned back to Aela, who continued to smile, and held up the wrecked portrait. In an almost inhuman voice he shouted, "Where is the map!"

Aela looked at the picture as if she was thoroughly shocked that the map wasn't there. "It's not there? I could have sworn…" She threw up her hands in an over exaggerated shrug and said, "Well, I guess we'll never really know."

This time nothing human came from the dark warlock's mouth, he roared in an almost demonic way and summoned his sword. He made to stab Aela, but I jumped in front of her and deflected his attack with my shield. The warlock stumbled back and shouted in gibberish, or at least that's what it sounded like, but it must have been one powerful spell because the whole top of the tower blew off and over our heads was a great black dragon.

"Well shoot," I said, gulping hard. "Look at that, he can summon a dragon at will. Tell me again why I came here?" I looked at Aela and said, "Oh yeah, now I remember."

I turned back to the warlock and saw that he was looking up at the dragon with a triumphant look on his face.

"Joe, you are just as strong as he is," Aela whispered.

I looked at her and somehow I knew what to do. I raised my sword and shouted the exact words that came from Morgar's mouth and… nothing happened.

Morgar looked at me and laughed an evil laugh, "You are far too weak to do such a powerful spell, boy." He continued to laugh and it was several harsh booms of laughter later that a ball of fire hit his dragon and sent it tumbling to the ground.

Morgar's head whipped around so fast that I thought maybe he had snapped his own neck, but his startled cry wasn't the result of any pain in his neck. Flying toward us was a giant blue dragon with red and white spikes running down his spine. It landed on the side of the tower and roared, shooting jets of red hot flames from its mouth.

"By Obcasus," Morgar said as a look of fear and amazement spread across on his face. "How is this possible?"

"Didn't you say you weren't going to underestimate me?" I asked with a grin.

"I will grind your bones…" Morgar started, but with a snap of my fingers the dragon whipped its tail at the wizard and sent him flying off the tower and down toward the fires from the explosions below.

"Hey, maybe we'll get lucky and one of his ribs will puncture his heart when he lands," I said hopefully.

"We may not be so lucky here," Aela said, walking up to the dragon. "I can't believe you actually summoned a dragon, Joe. That's very tough magic."

"What can I say?" I said with a winning smile. "I'm a class act!" Suddenly the sound of metal clanging on metal rang through the door and Aurora fell back, holding a zombie knight over her as it tried to press through to get to her. I ran over and grabbed the knight by the shoulders and tossed him up. The dragon belched out a tongue of flames and torched the zombie.

"Hey, you're just in time," I said, helping Aurora up to her feet. "We were just leaving!"

Aurora dusted herself off and looked up at the dragon and screamed. She brandished her sword at it as if that might scare it off.

As it were, however, the dragon just yawned and stared lazily at her, like it was trying to say, "Do we really have to do this?"

"Lower your sword, Aurora," I said, putting a hand on her blade. "He's a friend."

"A *friend*?" She exclaimed, looking overly confused. "How long was I down there fighting?"

"We should go," Aela called from across the room, she was looking over the side where Morgar had flown. "I think he's getting to his feet."

"Hey dragon," Aurora called to the winged lizard. "Care to give us a lift?"

The dragon gave her a look of contempt; he looked at me expectantly, waiting for orders.

"We could use a lift out of here, buddy," I said with a small smile. "Get us out of here, please?"

The dragon brought its lips up to show us his teeth, at first I thought he was growling at me, and then I realized the dragon was *smiling*. He lowered his head to allow us to climb on; I helped Aela up and stepped aside to let Aurora hop up on her own. I started to climb up onto the dragon and I felt something climbing up my leg, I looked down and saw Fives clambering up onto my shoulder. Within the past twenty four hours I have acquired a self-sufficient hand and a patriotic dragon, this adventure was getting really weird.

Once I was on, I gave the dragon the okay and he jumped off the tower. We all held on tightly as the dragon pumped its wings, and in minutes we were soaring high over the forest. I spun around; Aela had managed to sit herself between me and Aurora. She pulled out the parchment that she had nabbed before the dragons tore the place down. She unfolded it to reveal a map of Brindaria with a red line traced across it.

Aela puffed out a breath of relief. "I guess we're worthy. Alright, we're here," Aela said, pointing at a drawing of a castle. "And this," she pointed at a picture of a mountain that was topped with a crystal ball, "is where I'm assuming Merlin is hiding."

"*Assuming*," Aurora echoed.

"Yes," Aela said in an annoyed, tired tone. "I am basing this all on belief because that is all I have."

Aurora snorted and Aela sighed. I looked between the girls, so much like girls from my world; they probably wouldn't be at such odds if it weren't for one thing: me. I'm not an idiot, I can see when a girl is into me, and both of them are. And they know the other is into me and they're quarrel isn't over the existence of Merlin, I can tell that much.

I said, "Ladies, if we could get back to the task at hand here, please?" I looked at Aela and asked, "Which direction?"

"North-East," she said, pointing off in the distance.

"You heard her, big boy," I called to the dragon. "North-east."

This dragon must have had one great internal compass because he didn't even see where she pointed and he turned North-East and flew on.

"I've been thinking," Aela said thoughtfully.

"Uh oh," Aurora muttered.

Aela ignored her and went on, "We need to give this dragon a name instead of calling him 'the dragon.'"

"You're right," I said, rubbing the dragon's head. "What'll it be, bud?"

The dragon snorted, obviously as stumped as the rest of us. As we flew, Fives sat under my chin and rubbed it, as if he were in need of a chin to scratch in concentration. The answer was so obvious I didn't see why I didn't think of it before.

"We'll call him Captain," I said, smiling.

"Captain?" Aurora asked, looking confused.

"It's a, uh, Other-Realm thing," I said over my shoulder.

"Oh," she said, still sounding confused.

"I like it," Aela said, resting her head on my shoulder. "It sounds – how do they say in your world – groovy?"

Aurora groaned, probably rolling her eyes, but the Captain roared in approval. The roar echoed throughout the forest, and…

"Wait," I said, realizing something, "Why doesn't that echo sound like an echo?" I turned around and saw, to my horror, that we weren't the only things in the sky. The girls both turned and Aela screamed, and Aurora unsheathed her sword.

"Morgar is following us," Aela said, looking terrified.

"No," Aurora said. "There's no one on the dragon's back."

"So," I said in an upbeat voice, "good news is, a dragon is after us alone without the help of a warlock. The bad news is… a dragon is after us!"

"What do we do?" Aela asked, sounding worried.

"Well," I said, looking straight ahead, "we hold on tight."

"What?" Aurora asked.

"Captain," I said, steeling myself for what was about to happen, "evasive maneuvers."

Captain seemed to understand what I had said. He dived, narrowly escaping a fire ball, the likes of which saved us just minutes before. He pulled up before crashing into the trees and something told me I should get the girls to hang onto his spikes. I yelled for them to hang on and I grasped the spike in front of me, Aela wrapped her arms around my waist and Cap did a barrel roll, flipping one hundred and eighty degrees so that he was facing the other dragon. He unleashed a volley of fireballs at the black dragon and spun back around again. Captain shot forward like the fireballs he just unleashed and I could literally feel my skin pulling backwards.

Something hit my leg and sent a wave of pain up and I cried out, but to let go or look down at my leg would be suicide. We flew for a little while longer before Cap shook and let out a painful roar; I chanced a glance behind me and saw that he had been hit on his left wing. We started to lose altitude and I looked down to see a sea of trees.

The last thought that went through my mind before we crashed was, *Well this is going to hurt.*

Chapter 10

With a groan I awoke on the forest floor. I sat up dizzily and tried to stand, but the world did a somersault and I fell back down again. I blinked a few times, trying to focus. The pain in my leg was still there but it was the least of my problems, Captain was down and the girls were nowhere to be seen, judging by the fact that the sun hadn't moved since I last looked at it meant I was either out for a whole twenty four hours or I wasn't out for very long. Judging by the fact that we weren't surrounded by undead knights, I assumed it was the latter.

The world came to a slow rock, as if the massive waves rocking my boat had lessened. I was able to stand without falling over and I made my way toward the Captain. He didn't look like he was too badly injured aside from the burn on his left wing that caused us to drop. I looked to the sky as the black dragon circled above us, Morgar would be on his way soon.

"Aela?" I called, my echo ringing through the trees. "Aurora?"

"Well well well," came a sly voice that was dreadfully familiar. Two cat eyes and a big old yellow smile appeared out of thin air, followed by the floating body of a cat. Many other Faeles appeared behind the leader.

"I t'ought I taw a putty tat." I said in my best Tweety Bird impression.

"What?" the leader asked in a snarl.

"Nothing," I said, waving the question away. "What do you want, cat?"

"I want revenge," the cat said with a wicked smile. "Where is that wretched girl who pinned my compatriots to the trees?"

"I don't know," I said truthfully, though the cat didn't seem to believe me.

"Where is she, human?" The cat asked, I looked behind him and saw that the Captain was starting to get up.

"I'm telling you, I don't know, we got ambushed and we were split up."

"Forgive me," the cat said, floating toward me. "I don't believe you."

"Alright," I said, nodding my head. "If you don't believe me, why don't you ask *my* compatriot?" I pointed behind the cats and they all turned to see the Captain standing over them, teeth barred like a dog ready to strike.

"Oh," the lead Faeles said, frowning. "Well, you know, it's not that big of a deal. We can go look for her elsewhere." The cat whistled at his group and they all vanished in puffs of smoke.

"Thanks, Captain," I said, walking toward him. "Do you know where everyone is?"

The dragon snorted, shaking his head.

I sighed and looked around, Aela had the map and Aurora knew her way around a fight. I was utterly alone aside from Captain and Fives…

Fives. I realized I hadn't seen the little hand since the crash. I looked around widely, looking for him. The Cap must have known who I was looking for because he set out searching too. Eventually I noticed a pile of leaves rustling a few feet away, I ran to it and started to dig, a hand jutted out and I grabbed it. There was more than just a hand though; I pulled Aurora out of the leaves. She must have been hiding because she didn't look too dazed.

"Aurora," I said, pulling her to her feet. "What were you doing in there?"

"I woke up just before you," she explained, rubbing her head. "I heard the Faeles' voices and I knew they would want my head on a platter so I hid."

"Where's Aela?" I asked. "And Fives, do you know?"

She shook her head, "After we hit the trees everything got a little fuzzy. I didn't get knocked out but I was a little disoriented."

We both looked around for a good hour but with no more results than my first search. We sat down, leaning against Cap who threw a wing up over us for shade. I finally looked at my leg; I must have been hit by a rogue fireball because my whole calf was burned. I didn't know what to do, but apparently my body did. My hands rose to the burn and hovered over the wound, and I started speaking in the same gibberish that I had been speaking in to summon my dragon. I felt the skin on my leg tugging and pulling and finally it seemed to heal.

Aurora saw me do this and said, "It's strange, you being from the other world and being able to do the magic of this world."

"Yeah," I said, it was kind of weird. "I don't know how I do it sometimes; my body kind of just takes over and does it on its own."

Aurora got ready to say something, but then there was a rustling in the woods. Aurora and I hopped up, holding our swords at the ready and Captain growled menacingly.

Aela fell out from the tree line and landed on the ground, she was scratched up bad and looked as if she had gone for a swim.

"Aela!" I ran to the Princess, sheathing my sword, and I knelt down next to her, helping her up. "Are you alright?"

Aela looked up at me, still dazed, obviously. She said, "I'm fine. I was able to summon a pool of water to catch us before we slammed into the ground."

"Us?" Aurora asked, her sword still out.

Aela, who had been keeping a hand to her chest, moved it away to reveal Fives, looking as good as ever, as if he hadn't even fallen off a red, white, and blue dragon.

"We're all here," Aurora said nodding. "We should go."

"We'll have to walk," I said. "Captain's wing was severely burned in the air fight."

"Well then let's get moving," Aela said, pulling out the map. She had been marking our progress by landmark. "We have a lot of ground to cover."

We started walking, Captain was knocking tree after tree over as we went. We walked out into a clearing just as the sun started to dip behind the trees.

"Alright," I said, stopping and looking around the clearing. "I think we should stop for the night."

"Not a chance," Aurora said, pushing past me and crossing the clearing. "That dragon saw us land in the woods, and I am sure that it saw the trees Captain bumped into."

Captain huffed a plume of smoke from his nose and turned away from her.

"Come on," I said, grabbing her arm. "We can't just keep walking. We need to rest."

"I'll rest when I'm dead," Aurora said in a sweet tone. I looked to Aela for some help, but the Princess only shrugged and shook her head. I turned back to Aurora, who was already halfway across the clearing, and I sighed. I started to walk across the clearing when I heard the sound of wings, and I looked up just in time to see the black dragon swooping down on me. It grabbed me by the shoulders and hoisted me up.

I heard Aela scream from below and Captain roar, but the black dragon brought me up too high to hear much more. I looked up at the beast; it was scared and looked like it had been tortured to do as Morgar commanded, unlike Captain. It was determined; it looked like a child soldier from Sierra Leone: brainwashed, trained for nothing but bloodlust and killing. There would be no talking my way out of this, no getting through to it. I read *A Long Way Gone* in high school; I saw how long it took for the author to be fully rehabilitated.

No, to get out of this I had to fight, I had to slash and claw and do whatever I could to get out.

I took a deep breath, and I reached for my sword, and I brought it up to stab one of the claws holding my shoulders. The black dragon didn't bellow, but grunted, as if this pain was a mosquito bite compared to the pain it had taken in its tortures. Despite this, though, the dragon released my shoulder and I swung up and around, climbing up its leg and hopped up onto its shoulder.

The dragon turned its head to blast me with a jet of flames but I hopped to the side and slashed its left eye. That got me a nice loud roar. I made to stab the dragon in the mouth as it roared, but the dragon was good, it rolled to the left, as if to drop me from its back. I managed to jump beforehand and I brought my sword down into the dragon's chest. The dragon bellowed and shot flames from its mouth and nostrils as it started to disintegrate in shadows.

I realized my mistake too late, and I started to fall through the shadow of the dragon I had just slain. I plummeted toward the clearing and – despite my desire to look as manly as possible – I screamed like a little girl. I knew I was going to die and there wasn't much I could do about it, but my body never gives up. My mouth went from screaming to chanting in that tongue I was never taught and soon my descent began to slow until I was at a complete stand still.

I looked around, I was *flying*; the one superpower I would have loved to have more than anything. I knew I had no time for play around with this, so I started to lower myself slowly back into the clearing. When I finally touched down in the center of the clearing, the rest of the group was standing there waiting.

I looked at Aurora and said, "We'll rest."

Aurora looked at me like I was more than just eye candy; she looked at me as if I were someone greater, someone to respect and someone to fear.

She nodded her head and said, "We'll rest."

I went to get wood to start a fire while Captain went down onto his belly and closed his eyes to sleep. I walked to the edge of the clearing and started to pick up loose branches and fallen twigs. As I collected, I started thinking, once we got to Merlin's mountain, what then? We just let the old wizard take over and go home and wait it out? I was thinking about what to say to Merlin to convince him to let us help when someone came up behind me.

I turned around to see Aela walking softly toward me. She stopped beside me and started to pick up branches along with me. We hadn't really had a chance to talk about what happened before I was pulled into that mirage. We didn't even really have a chance to talk about Arec.

"Aela," I started but she stopped me before I could say anything else.

"It can't happen, Joe," She said. "You and I, we're not from the same world. It just can't work."

"Aela," I tried again, but once more she cut me off.

"I only kissed you because I thought it was the last time I would ever see you. I never anticipated…"

"Aela," I said, a lot more firmly this time. "Listen to me, there's a lot I don't understand right now. Why I'm able to do the things I do, why I felt so apt to joining you on this little adventure, but the one thing that I *do* know," I grabbed her hands, "is that if I'm going to die, I'm going to die for something worthwhile, with *someone* worthwhile."

She looked me in the eyes, trying to find some indication whether or not I was just saying that or if I truly meant it. She was about to say something, but Aurora must have been bored with the love show because she called from across the field, "Brr, I'm *sooo* cold!"

Aela and I both sighed, we both picked up the firewood we had dropped and started to walk back. When we got there, I stacked up the wood so that I could start a fire, and then those words came to my mouth in that odd possessed way it did. Soon we were sitting in the orange glow of a camp fire. I turned to Captain and got to work on mending the wing that had been damaged in the air fight, it wasn't as bad as it had seemed at first; the fireball had barely grazed it. Unfortunately, it had been so hot that the burn was bad enough that I had to spend most of the night mending it. When I was done, the moon was just reaching its pinnacle in the sky. I looked to Aurora, who had been switching watches with Aela while I worked, and she nodded to me, indicating that I could sleep and that she would wake Aela in an hour for the next two hour watch.

I laid down and closed my eyes, but I was asleep before my eyelids were fully closed.

Chapter 11

I was flying high over the forest, watching the sea of trees go by. The picture shifted and I saw Morgar flying on thin air, probably using the same spell that saved my life earlier that day. He had a look of pure resentment on his face; he wasn't happy. He must have known I killed his precious dragon, because behind him was a flock of evil looking birds. They were all black with long necks and beaks filled with razor sharp teeth. They had a wing span almost that of an eagle or a hawk. When they flapped they let out screeches, the likes of which I had never heard before, and I hope I never will again.

Morgar and his birds were still at least a day's flight away from us; they were just now reaching our crash site. Morgar slowed to a hover and looked down at where we had hit the trees, probably looking for a sign of someone's death. He mustn't have found anything, though, because he cursed and flew on.

"Remember, birds," Morgar shouted over his shoulder. "I want the Princess *alive* but the other two... well, I *have* been neglecting to feed you lately."

The birds screeched in a way that I assumed was pleasure at the fact that their bellies would soon be full. Morgar smiled for the first time in the vision, he knew he was close...

Chapter 12

I woke with a start, knowing that we had no time to lose. The sun had begun to peak over the horizon that the trees blocked from view, so all we had to go on was the glow that emanated through the trees. Aela and Aurora were getting a small breakfast together, Aela must have gone hunting, Aurora not being able to kill and all.

I got up and told them about my dream, and Aela looked concerned. At first I thought she was concerned about Morgar but she said, "How long have you been having visions like these?"

"I don't know," I said, trying to recall. "That night before we came here I did have some kind of vision. I must have been in Morakâr in that dream, because I met Obcasus." That seemed to send a chill through the group, even Fives had stopped fidgeting to listen to the story.

"Why didn't you tell me or…" Aela stopped, I knew she was going to say Arec, but instead she said, "… or Aurora this sooner?"

"Because, I just thought I was having a dream then, you know? I didn't think about it being real until after *this* vision."

"We should get going," Aurora said, saving my hide and bringing Aela back to the problem at hand. "What do you say, dragon, you all set to go?"

Captain gave his wing a little flapping test, sending a powerful gust of wind in our direction. The dragon seemed satisfied because he grinned in that dragon-like way and gave a joyous roar. We all smiled and I helped the ladies on first and then I let Fives scuttle up to my shoulder. I climbed on Captain's back and up we went, flying toward Merlin's Mountain. According to Aela, we would arrive later in the evening if we spent the whole day flying and we didn't get "delayed."

Luckily nothing delayed our journey any more than it had to. We arrived at Merlin's Mountain just as the sun was setting. We all decided that we shouldn't stop here, it would be dark in the mountains whether we waited until morning or not. So Captain landed on a ledge next to a cave entrance and we all walked in.

I found a stick lying on the ground and I lit the tip, and then I led the team further in. We walked mostly in silence, lest there be some monster lurking in the dark, but there was nothing. I tried to ignore the claustrophobic feeling of being trapped like rats if someone were to follow us in. I was confident Captain could stop most of anything at the entrance where we left him, but if Morgar arrived before we could get to Merlin I feared the old dragon would be no match.

We stopped at the end of the corridor, where I expected there to be an amazingly large magical door. Instead, we found a decrepit looking wooden door that was rotting away.

"Well that's highly anticlimactic," I said with a frown.

"Well I guess it makes sense," Aela said. "If there were any adventurers do you think they'd want to go in *there*?"

"I don't even want to go in *now*," Aurora said with a tone of disgust.

"Well too bad," I said, and I reached for the knob. The minute I touched the bronze doorknob the whole door started to glow until an amazing sight stood before us.

The amazingly large magical door I was hoping for appeared at my touch; I looked at the girls and grinned wide. I pushed through the door and walked into a large room filled with remarkable things.

There were telescopes and star charts; tables with potions and poisons; bookshelves wrapped around the room *full* of what I assumed were spell books. And in the center of the room was a crystal ball, and on that ball was a piece of parchment. We walked over to the crystal ball and I looked at the parchment.

To whom it may concern,

Welcome to my glorious little hide away, in here you will find magic like you wouldn't believe. Only I am powerful enough to work this paraphernalia, but that also means you *are powerful enough as well Joseph. Touch the crystal ball, and you will understand everything.*

Mystically yours,
Merlin

"What does he mean that *I'm* powerful enough after saying that only he is?" I asked, curious.

"What I want to know," Aurora said suspiciously, "is how he knew you would be here."

"I guess there's only one way to find out," I said, reaching for the crystal ball. A loud roar came from outside, and I felt a pain in my chest. "Captain," I said, hesitating over the crystal ball.

"Joe, you have to do it," Aela said, drawing her sword. "Grab it!"

"But the Captain," I said, the pain still in my chest.

"Oh for the love of…" Aurora said, she grabbed my arm and pushed down, causing me to touch the crystal. Everything around me faded to black just as Morgar came barging into the room.

Chapter 13

Information swirled around my head like crazy; spells, people, personalities. Everything started to make sense now.

After Merlin had trapped Obcasus in Morakâr he vanished. What nobody knew, however, was that he didn't vanish into thin air or into the woods to live in the wild. Merlin opened a portal into the other realm and lived his life. Then he grew old and started over again, and again, and again until he was born under the name Joseph Wallace Christian.

Merlin is me, I am Merlin. We're one in the same person. Merlin left his consciousness here where he was able to watch over this world while his body lived throughout the ages in the other realm. He was never anyone important, just your average Joes with no real value. When Merlin's consciousness saw that Morgar had possessed the king, he unlocked the abilities that were locked away in his body… in me.

Now, touching the crystal ball, the knowledge of Merlin and every memory the guy had was pumped into my skull. For a normal person, this would be too much, but I had the body and brain of Merlin.

Don't let Morgar raise Obcasus, Joe. Came an elderly voice in the void. *You have the power to stop him...*

Chapter 14

When I snapped back to the present, I was disoriented for a moment. When I finally focused, it was a disaster area. The bookshelves were bare and burned, the potions were splattered on the walls and floor, and the telescopes were bent and snapped. Aurora was on the floor across the room and Fives was hanging from a stalactite above, and Aela was… gone.

I ran over to Aurora just as she was starting to wake up. I helped her to her feet and asked her what had happened.

"Well," she started, rubbing her head, "after you touched that ball and went into that odd trance, Morgar arrived with a flock of very angry birds. When he saw you, Morgar told the birds to attack the Princess and me while he took care of you. So the birds started to attack us and Morgar went after you, but when he tried to touch you there was an explosion that sent him hurtling backwards. When he recovered he told the birds to take me out and grab Aela, so the birds swarmed me and I fell to the ground and feigned death. It was all I could do to survive, not knowing if you'd be back with us in time to help."

"We need to save her," I said, anger swelling up inside me. Not only because of Morgar, but because of myself as well. "Come on, we can't waste any time."

"Wait," Aurora said, grabbing my arm. "What happened with you over there?"

"I learned a few things about myself," I said simply. "Come on, we have no time to lose."

"What about Merlin?" Aurora asked, chasing after me, Fives jumped down and landed on my shoulder.

"What about him?" I asked, not looking back at her.

"Well, if worse comes to worst we're going to need him," Aurora said.

"No we won't," I said as I ran through the magical doorway. We sprinted along to the entrance of the cave and I saw, to my dismay, that Captain was nowhere in sight.

"Why won't we need the most powerful wizard in all of Brindaria?" Aurora asked skeptically.

"Because," I said, finally turning to Aurora, "I'm Merlin."

"You're Merlin?" Aurora asked as if it were the most ludicrous thing she had ever heard.

"Yes," I said, "I'm Merlin." I explained to her everything I saw when I touched that crystal ball, and explained every little detail about how Merlin had pulled it off. Aurora must have seen that I was telling the truth because her expression shifted.

"You really are him, aren't you?" She asked in awe.

"Yes," I said. "Well, no. I'm him in the sense of his mortal body, but *his* consciousness is still in that ball. He unlocked the knowledge of all the spells he knew in *my* brain, though. I'm just as strong as he had been when he shoved Obcasus into Morakâr."

"Well let's get back to Morgar's castle before you have to put that to the test," Aurora said.

"Right," I said, nodding. "Well, hold on tight. We're going to need to fly long and hard to make up for lost time."

"Fly?" Aurora asked nervously. "How? Captain is gone, we have no way of flying."

"What's the good of being the most powerful wizard in the world if I can't do this," I said, and I started to chant in that gibberish that I still don't understand. Soon there was the sound of beating wings, and a roar shook the mountain. A red, white, and blue dragon landed on the ledge beside us, roaring proudly.

"Oh my," Aurora said, taken aback.

I looked back at her with a grin, "You didn't think losing the dragon was as simple as that, did you? It takes one specific spell that I doubt Morgar knows to permanently kill a dragon."

I helped the assassin onto Captain and climbed on myself, and then Captain let out a tremendous roar and took off south-west, toward Morgar's Castle. I knew it was going to be dangerous, and I even knew that it might be impossible to actually prevent what was about to happen, but as long as I stopped Obcasus that was all that mattered. Or at least it should have been, but I still had the urge to save Aela before that happened...

Chapter 15

We were flying for about half an hour before I could see Morgar's castle over the horizon. The fires had been put out and the knights were at work rebuilding the tower that had been torn off by Morgar's black dragon. The aforementioned dragon sat perched on another tower watching more knights building a sacrificial shrine.

"That shrine will be used to raise Obcasus," I said, pointing at the shrine.

"It's not even done yet," Aurora said with a hint of hope in her voice.

"The shrine is just for looks," I said, shaking my head. "As long as Morgar has the Key of Morakâr and Aela he'll be able to bring Obcasus back."

"Oh," she said and I could hear the hope leaving her voice.

I told the Captain to land a mile away from the castle, and when he touched down Aurora and I started walking. We made it about half a mile across the field when I sensed something behind us and I stopped. I whipped around, sword in hand, to find an army of floating cats following behind.

"Can we not do this right now, Faeles?" I asked impatiently. "I have somewhere to be."

"It's true," the leader of the cats said in awe. "Merlin is upon us." Many of the cats gasped while others "oohed" and "ahhed".

"That's right," I said. "So don't mess with me because I am *not* in the mood right now."

"You get us wrong, Lord Merlin," the leader said in an apologetic tone. "We mean to join you in your venture to save the Princess."

"Why should we trust *you*?" Aurora asked sternly. "You tried to kill all of us at one point or another."

"That was before Merlin returned and the light returned to our hearts," the leader said. "We *never* would have believed that Merlin would rise in time to stop Morgar from raising Obcasus."

"It could be a trick," Aurora warned me.

"Yes," I said, nodding, "yes it could… but I don't believe that's what this is."

"What?" Aurora asked in shock while the leader of the cats seemed to have the weight of the world pulled off of his shoulders.

"It's like with Fives here," I explained. "They're pack was like a body possessed by darkness. With the return of Merlin, however, the light has returned to the heart of their body."

"Exactly," the leader cat said, nodding wildly. "Please, allow us the honor of fighting by your side."

"Alright," I said, nodding. "Come on, let's save ourselves a Princess."

We all charged the castle; the knights were taken aback and overpowered within the first few minutes of fighting. I didn't even wait for the rest of my army; I said some gibberish and flew up to the top of the tower.

When I reached the top, I found Aela chained to the floor like Princess Leia in Star Wars.

"Aela," I said, walking to her. She started to stir, and when she sat up, I saw that the key was right under her.

"Joe?" The Princess said uncertainly. Her eyes went wide with horror, and I turned to see Morgar floating above me.

"Well," Morgar said deviously. "Look who we have here. Well, amateur magician, I don't know how you pulled off that force field, but this time I have you right where I want you."

"I think you have it the wrong way, Morgar," I said grinning. "*I* have *you* right where I want you."

"What?" Morgar snapped, and right on cue Captain flew up behind him. Morgar turned in time to see the dragon roar. He screamed and turned back to me and, summoning his magic sword, he threw it at me just as the dragon's great jaws clamped down on him. I moved aside and the sword flew past me, I turned to the dragon and nodded at him.

"Great job, Cap," I said. I turned back to Aela, and to my dismay I saw that the sword that I had dodged had found its way to her, the sword stuck through her chest and her blood trickled down her body and onto… the Key of Morakâr.

"No," I said as the clouds started to thicken and grow darker. Lightning crackled and the earth began to quake and crack, and in the middle of the courtyard the ground caved in. From that hole rose a demonic creature that I had only seen once… in my dreams.

"I am risen," Obcasus boomed in a monstrous voice. The demonic beast turned to look at me and smiled a wicked evil grin. He spoke in a voice that made my hair stand up straight on my neck, "Ah, my old foe, you shall not defeat me this time."

"We'll see about that," I said angrily. I sent a volley of fire balls at the demon, but he brushed if off as if I had shot a spit ball at him. The beast chuckled and sent his own volley of fire at me; I grabbed Aela and pulled her off the tower with me just as the fire balls crashed into the stone building. I said some gibberish so that we landed safe and sound, or as safe as we could be with the devil standing five hundred feet over us.

"I have developed abilities that you would never believe while imprisoned in that… that… well, I guess *Hell* would be the perfect word to use to describe it. That Hell that you trapped me in." Obcasus spoke in the same gibberish that I had been speaking, except I didn't know these words, which means Merlin didn't know these words. The sky turned blood red and flaming rocks began to rain down on Brindaria. Even the Army of the Dead wasn't safe from this maelstrom.

"None shall live as I reign over this world," Obcasus boomed. "You shall *all* die under my fists." The Captain flew up to him and bit the giant's hand. Obcasus bellowed and with a flick of his wrist and the uttering of some gibberish, Cap vanished in a puff of smoke. Satan had used the spell to banish a dragon for all of eternity…

"*No!*" I shouted. I started speaking in all sorts of gibberish until I started to grow, and grow, and grow, until I was the same height as Obcasus. "You bastard," I said, my face glowing red with anger.

"Ooh," Obcasus said deviously. "You learned a thing or two since the last time I saw you, Joseph. Let's see how much you have learned." Obcasus shouted a few words of gibberish and multiple black swords appeared over his shoulders, all blades trained on me. The blades shot forward and I held up the shield that Arec had made for me. Some of the blades bounced off my shield, but two of them found their way around. One sliced my leg while another caught me on the side. I grunted as I lowered the shield, the blades had vanished on contact; I took that as my turn.

I said some gibberish and suddenly there was a rumbling all around. Obcasus looked around for the source of the rumbling when suddenly the ground beneath his feet opened up and he was swallowed by a giant sandworm.

I grinned, thinking about the movie Beetlejuice and how convenient that spell had been. I knew it couldn't be *that* easy to beat this guy, which was why I wasn't surprised when a hole in the ground exploded into existence and Obcasus climbed out.

He was bleeding, which definitely brought up my spirits, if it could bleed it could die. Obcasus stood and wiped the blood from his lips and grinned a bloody grin.

"Well," he said, specks of blood hopping from his mouth, "I had forgotten the feel of pain and the sensation of blood. You pose a very interesting foe, Christian."

"In the other realm imagination is all a man has," I said, smiling back at him. "And in that aspect, I'm probably the most dangerous in the world."

"Well then it's a good thing I am not a man," Obcasus said grimly.

"True," I said, nodding. "But you also don't know anything about my world, which means you don't know any of the imaginative things people have come up with!" I said some more gibberish and an anvil dropped on the demon's head. The word Acme was written on the side and I laughed as I did when I saw the same thing on an episode of Looney Tunes.

"What was *that*?" Obcasus asked, throwing the anvil away.

"Just a little taste of my world," I said.

"If you think petty tomfoolery will be enough to defeat me you are sadly mistaken, my boy," Obcasus snarled. He directed a flaming rock toward me and I wasn't fast enough to dodge it, it hit me and I flew backwards into the woods. With my current size it was like falling onto a bunch of Legos, I landed hard on top of pine, oak, maple, and any other type tree you can think of.

I groaned, knowing that this was going to take a lot more than just cheap cartoon tricks. I needed a plan, a good plan before Obcasus found a way to finish me off for good.

Then I remembered something from earlier in our adventure, something that had kept me trapped long enough for Morgar to do some serious damage. I shouted some gibberish and I vanished into thin air, it was a spell Merlin had developed *after* he had thrown Obcasus into Morakâr so he shouldn't know what I did. I snuck around and started to chant something, and then I appeared directly behind Obcasus and shouted, "Hey ugly!"

Obcasus whipped around and saw me; he smiled and started to walk toward me. I brandished my sword and Obcasus made a sword much like Morgar's appear. He charged at me and I got into a defensive position. Obcasus crashed into me and vanished, leaving a ripple as if he had run into a wall of water.

I changed the image so that I could see him; he was floating in a black void.

Obcasus cracked a smile and boomed, "Very nice trick, Christian, but you can't hold me in an illusion such as this." Obcasus started to chant and when he finished his smile twisted into an ugly grimace. "What manner of spell craft is this, eh?"

"A Mirage," I said, amplifying my voice into the void. I watched the horror slowly develop on Obcasus' face as he realized how royally screwed he was. And then there was a sound, a clacking and screeching. Obcasus looked around wildly, as if looking for whatever the darkness held, even the devil was afraid of the dark. And then little creatures appeared, they were a simple kind of horrifying. They were small and round and when they opened their mouths they revealed rows and rows of sharp little teeth that moved around like the chain of a chainsaw.

"No!" Obcasus screamed as the Mirage Monsters started to fillet the man, because that's all he was… a man.

I disbanded the Mirage, trapping him in void to be eaten alive. I turned around as I began to shrink and I was met by Aurora, who had sprinted from the castle to meet me; she was followed by the leader of the Faeles, who was beginning to look less and less hostile. His hair started to mat back down to his body and his murderous eyes began to look a lot friendlier. And when the cat smiled there were no sharp, menacing teeth, but even rows of pearly whites, which I still found odd for a cat, but who am I to question this place?

"Joe, you did it," Aurora said, smiling a real smile; something I have never seen from her.

"Yeah," I said, smiling a little. I looked over to where I had left Aela's body and to my horror I saw that Fives was trying to fend off a man who I had thought to be dead. I charged to Fives' aid, drawing my sword. When Morgar looked up he simply smiled and flicked his wrist, but when nothing happened, the sneer he was wearing twisted into a confused scowl. When he heard my chanting he realized what I was doing. It was too late for him to do anything about it, though. I put a hand on his forehead and another where his heart should be and felt a pulse transfer through me. The wizard's body crumpled into dust as if he had been a corpse untouched by the air for thousands of years.

I turned to see Fives twitching and writhing, I realized I had made a huge mistake, in killing Morgar I had killed everything of his. The zombies were all collapsing, the eerie castle grounds began to gain more color and life, and Fives – Morgar's hand – was starting to crumple to dust. I fell to my knees, wracking my brain for a spell that could stop this but I couldn't think of anything. Fives waved to me, his final good bye, and then he crumpled to dust with the rest of Morgar's remains.

I wiped the tears from my face and got to my feet, I walked over to Aela, who was laying just a few feet away.

The sword that stabbed her had vanished when Morgar was killed. She was bleeding out, and I knew the spell to save her; I just had to utter the simple words to bring her back, but something stopped me. Something in me told me that I should bring her back; it wasn't her time, she didn't deserve to die. But there was a small voice in the back of my head that kept saying, *you can't play God. Who are you to decide who lives and who dies?* I listened to that voice, for I knew that it was the voice of reason, the voice of Merlin seeping into my mind from his mountaintop across the land of Brindaria.

So all I did was lift the Princess up and carry her towards the woods. Away from Aurora and the cats, away from this damned castle where Aela had met her bitter end. I carried her to the place where we had shared more than just a quest; I carried her to the place where our friend was buried. When I arrived at that clearing, I could see Arec's headstone, and I laid her down on the ground at the foot of his grave, and I started to dig next to the mound of dirt.

When the digging was done, I lowered her in and kissed her forehead. I laid her hands on her stomach and climbed out of the hole. From here she looked like Sleeping Beauty, she could have been sleeping aside from the hole in her middle. I had placed her hands over the wound as if to block the ugly gash from the world. She deserved to die as beautifully as she lived, and I wanted to give her that.

I buried her and put a rock at the head of the grave and etched into the rock's face,

Rest in peace, Aela.
Princess.
Friend.
Hero.

Chapter 16

I stayed in that clearing all night, and when the sun started to rise again I heard a rustling in the woods. No one could sneak up on me though, not with my newfound magical abilities.

"What is it, Aurora?" I called over my shoulder.

I heard footsteps behind me and Aurora said, "How are you doing, Merlin?"

"Oh just great," I said sarcastically. "I just defeated the most evil being in the history of evil guys and what do I get? I lose the one person that showed even the vaguest interest in being with me."

"Oh suck it up, wizard," the assassin said, kneeling beside me. "It's not the end of the world. There are plenty of women out there for you, I'm sure. Besides, after you touched that crystal ball you became the most powerful, and thus the most attractive, man in this realm *and* yours."

"Thanks, Aurora," I said, nodding. "Really, that makes me a feel a lot better."

Aurora smiled a sweet smile, which looked kind of odd on *her* face. It was strange, out of everyone I never thought the last friend I'd have in this realm would be the Assassin Who Couldn't Kill. And that's when it hit me…

"Aurora," I said. "We're friends, right?"

"Yeah," Aurora said, looking confused.

"Well, because you helped me, not out of a selfish gain in the end. But because you wanted to help us…"

"I don't know what you're talking about," Aurora said convincingly.

"You can't lie to me," I said and then I continued, "Because you helped us in this I've decided to do something for you." I got up and pulled her to her feet, I put one hand on her head and another on her heart, much like I did with Morgar, but this time I wasn't killing.

I started to chant under my breath and Aurora gasped as a pulse of energy went through me and into her.

The assassin stumbled back, gasping. "What did you just do?"

I smiled and used a little bit of my magic to guide a deer out into the clearing and I pointed at it. "Aim and fire," I said. "Shoot to kill."

Aurora looked aghast, "You know I cannot do that, Joe."

"Aim," I said simply. "And fire. Shoot to kill."

Aurora groaned, she notched an arrow and fired but I stopped it in midflight.

"I asked for a kill shot. Stop aiming for minor wounds."

Aurora looked at me pleadingly. She notched another arrow and fired without taking her eyes off me, the deer dropped dead.

I looked at the arrow sticking out of the deer's eye and said, "Nice shot."

I looked back at the assassin to see that she still had her eyes on me, tears streaming down her cheeks. I couldn't tell if she was angry at me or if she was happy. So when she dropped the bow and arrow and walked up to me, I was still wary of a dagger poking into my gut. Instead, though, she wrapped her arms around my neck and hugged me close, I could hear her quiet sobs as she cried into my shoulder.

"Thank you," she whispered into my ear. "Thank you *so* much."

And so the Assassin Who Could Kill and I walked back to the castle of Brindaria arm in arm.

Chapter 17

We stood within the throne room of the castle, neither of us taking a seat in the throne. They weren't our seats, though we didn't know who would rule the Kingdom of Brindaria now that all of the royal family was dead. We looked around the wrecked room; Morgar had really done a number on this place.

"So what will you do now, Warlock?" Aurora asked, looking around the throne room.

"I'll return home," I said. "I'll write about this, I'll make people know that all of this is real."

"Would you consider allowing Brindaria access to your world?" Aurora asked curiously.

"No," I said. "If I've learned anything while being here, it's that this world doesn't need my world, it's the other way around. Back when all of this was believable in my world things were good and happy. Now no one believes in magic, they rely on machines to do everything for them. That can't happen in this world, to let that happen could eventually kill everything the people of Brindaria know." Aurora looked both disappointed and grateful with that. "What about you, Aurora? What are you going to do?"

"I don't know," Aurora said. "I was thinking about going back into the old game."

"Assassins don't get paid nearly as much as Generals," came a voice behind us. We both turned to see a stout man waddling toward them.

"Who are you?" Aurora asked, raising her bow, but I put my hand out to block her.

"Aurora," I said, kneeling. "This is the Dwarf King."

"Aye," the dwarf said chuckling. "Stand up, Warlock. You need not bow to me, it should be me bowing to you."

"No," I said, standing. "There's no need to bow to me."

"You are Merlin, are you not?"

"Well yeah," I started.

"Then bow I shall," the Dwarf King said, kneeling before me. "Without you this world would be nothing but ash."

"You said something about a general?" I asked, trying to change the subject.

"Aye," the king said, grunting as he stood again. He turned to Aurora and said, "I would be honored to have one as gifted in a fight as you in my army, Aurora Hayfield."

"Maybe the reign of man in Brindaria is over," I said, smiling. "Maybe this land should go back to the ones who inhabited it before man arrived."

"You would relinquish control back to the Dwarves?" the king asked.

"A good friend of mine was a dwarf; he made me this armor without which I never would have been able to stop Obcasus. I trusted that dwarf with my life; I think I can trust the rest of his race with this nation."

"Thank you, Warlock," the dwarf king said, bowing again.

"Don't mention it," I said, smiling.

"But I must mention it if anyone is to believe that dwarves are to rule Brindaria," the king said, confused.

"Nevermind," I said, shaking my head. "Just an expression. I should be going, though. This world isn't in need of Merlin anymore, but maybe my world could use a touch of magic."

"You're leaving," Aurora said sadly. She stuck out her hand and I took it in mine, we shook firmly as I smiled at her.

"Listen," I said, "you be good here; I'll pop in every now and again when I can."

"Alright," Aurora said, smiling.

"Your highness," I said, nodding to the Dwarf King.

"Warlock," the king said, returning my nod.

I turned on my heel and walked out of the castle, I said a quick spell of gibberish and flew north east, toward Merlin's Mountain; there was something I needed to get my hands on. When I got to the mountain I walked into the cave and down the cavern hall to the magical door that was hanging on its hinges. I fixed it with magic and walked inside. With a wave of my hand the room put itself back together, undoing all the destruction that Morgar caused. Then I approached what I had gone for, the Crystal Ball.

I picked it up – it was lighter than you'd expect – and I put it into a bag that I had gotten from the castle. I turned and walked out of the room. When I stepped through the door, it closed and turned back into the old fashioned wooden door as I left the cave. I stood at the end of the cliff and chanted, clapped my hands over my head, making an echo across the mountain range, and then there was black.

Chapter 18

I opened my eyes to find myself back outside my house. There were a lot of cars in my driveway, and I recognized Colin, Kristen, and Kate's cars. I walked inside to find everyone sitting in my living room, watching the news. The news showed the Mall of New Hampshire back to its old self, no giant shroud of dark energy covering it.

Everyone looked up at the sudden entrance and when they saw me, still in my "Sir Captain of America" armor, they all jumped up and ran to me. I had fought floating cats, dragons, and even Satan himself, but I still couldn't hold my ground against these people: my friends and family, as they tackled me in a hug. They all asked about my adventures, so instead of telling them I had them gather around my crystal ball as I placed it on the coffee table.

As we watched the past few days unfurl in the crystal ball I had an idea. I let everyone finish watching my adventure, and when it was done I hung around for a little while until my friends left. I grabbed my laptop and went into my room and started to write…

Epilogue

As I sit here now, watching myself walk into the bedroom and sit in this very spot, I've come to see how fortunate I was to have the life I lived.

Seeing all the death, losing three people who came to mean a lot to me, it was hard. But seeing that magic and everything I had heard about was real was a fantastic feeling. And coming to find that I was essentially the "Father of Magic" was as great a feeling as any.

I think about everyone I lost on the way to find this power locked away inside of me.

Arec; he was a tough little man, always trying to be as protective as he could.

The Captain; he was there when I needed him. He was my first big spell, the first look into what I'd be capable of.

Fives; he had been my right hand… hand.

And of course there was Aela, who couldn't have meant more to me if she tried.

Without those people, I never would have made it through that mess; I doubt that I would have even survived. The crystal ball shimmered and showed an image of my family and friends from *this* world, showing me who I had been fighting for all along.

My mother and father, my brother and sister. Kate, Kristen, and Colin and all of the other people I had gotten close to over the years. I fought for their safety, and the safety of everyone else in this world *and* in Brindaria.

I'm not writing this as a way to get noticed, I don't want people worshipping me or calling me God. I am writing this to give back to the people what they deserve: Faith. Magic is real, and it's all around us but we're so blinded by television and video games that we don't see it. With my abilities, though, you better believe the world will start believing again.

My name is Joe Christian, and I am a Wizard.